# DEDICATION

To all the people who influenced me from 2012 to 2016, for better or for worse. This story is my love letter to you all.

# CONTENTS

# PREFACE

This story was my second attempt at a National Novel Writing Month challenge, and the first that I completed within the time allotted. The precursor to *Outer Darkness* was a short story I had written for myself called "The Contract," which was a personal challenge to create a work of fiction based on my life after the manner of Franz Kafka: the entrapment of a hapless protagonist, the surreal bureaucracy, the tragic ending, and even the unintentional sense of camp I find in some English translations of his literature. Writing "The Contract" was a neat little experiment (and a way to vent frustration), but I decided to revisit some of the themes in a less confined literary style.

That said, my initial outline for *Outer Darkness* went through several revisions: changes were made to blur the parallels between people in my waking life and characters in my novel, names were consistently altered until I found ones that fit, plot elements were altered to focus more on the supernatural rather than the cynical, and so forth. One of the most notable changes was the addition of the first chapter's events, which began as a fan fiction idea for a video game I was obsessed with at the time. (This is why a certain character dons a purple sweatshirt.) Despite all of my preparation, I still went into NaNoWriMo half-cocked and made drastic storyline edits, such as the addition of Armin and the combination of two chapters, to keep things moving.

Although this novel is essentially a *roman à clef* detailing events in my life from the end of 2012 to exactly four years later, I stand by my insistence that all of the people in this story are composite characters. After all, I am sure that most of the people around me would be less than thrilled if I used their personas as the basis for my novel's many antagonists, and even worse if I used them as love interests. Likewise, the nameless church in *Outer Darkness* is based on my real-life experiences as a convert to a fringe denomination of Christianity—I decided against identifying the church by name to avoid a lawsuit, but I hope that those who have had similar experiences can identify with Lenore's spiritual struggle. It is because of all the parallels that I was initially hesitant to publish *Outer Darkness*, but writing Lenore's story has been therapeutic for me in my time of need. I knew that having a hard copy of the novel in my hand would legitimize my tale, even if I was the only one who would ever read it, so seeing this story go to print was a necessary evil.

The concept of "outer darkness" resonated with me as a metaphor for existing outside of the bureaucratic demands of religion, and by association, of romantic relationships. (Incidentally, the mention of outer darkness in the Bible is found in a parable about a wedding feast.) Although meant to symbolize hell or the home of the sons of perdition, I imagined it as an escape from the ideas about mankind's views of heaven, where worthy souls would end up in divine servitude or a continuation of their miserable but obedient lives on Earth. I figured that no loving God would create a unique, sentient being only to destroy it, so I decided that in this version of the afterlife, even those in outer darkness would not be subject to eternal damnation. On a similar note, I have always disliked the fictional representations of heaven created by the likes of Jack T. Chick and the *Left Behind* authors that have somehow crept into the canon of modern-day Christianity. If God works in mysterious and humble ways, why should I believe that he would burst into this world with fanfare and chaos? Why not a silent apocalypse, where people are unaware of their fate and impending judgment until after the fact? Why not believe that God would call upon his children individually and personally, when he found them to be worthy? If nothing else, at least it is a different idea.

I would like to thank everyone who inspired this story—whether portrayed in a positive or negative light—and the few people who still support me after the numerous mistakes and trials I have dived headfirst into over the years. Please enjoy my novel.

Sarah Elaine Ranly

# CHAPTER ONE

The night of December 21, 2012 was predicted to be the day the world would end by one Christian denomination or another, or perhaps the Mayans. Nevertheless, few people, if any, were taking that bit of information into account on that date. Most people either laughed about the impending doomsday, or outright ignored it, or were completely unaware. This was especially true of those people who were already lost to their own Armageddon, particularly the hedonistic youth who were paving the way for their own hedonistic demise.

One such group of young adults was actually on their way to a nearby nightclub on the alleged eve of destruction. The Edge of Heaven nightclub was a popular 1980s-themed hangout that those millennials had yet to visit, and it was one of the rare nights where the entire group was available to meet up together. The leader of the pack was John DeLuna, a dark-complexioned ectomorph with close-cropped black hair and narrow eyes. He sat behind the wheel of his black Mustang convertible in a dark blue Metallica muscle shirt, one hand resting on the steering wheel and the other poised over the clutch, ready to exceed the speed limit at a moment's notice. Sitting shotgun was his girlfriend of four months, Lenore Kavaranian, a petite olive-skinned beauty, her chin-length black hair topped with a vinyl commander's cap and thick eyebrows covered by a straight line of fringe. She gazed jadedly out toward the expanse of hills, sweeping by in a blur, while the rest of the gang quipped and blathered in the back seat about things they had done in the absence of each other: a trip to Applebee's for liquor shots, a night at the bar playing pool and dancing to "Gangnam Style," and other such outings that made Lenore regret not having more money to be able to do things with her friends.

Matt, the token Anglo-Saxon of the group, finally addressed Lenore directly. "So Lenore," he called out in his jovial tenor voice, "What adventures have you been on in the last month?"

Lenore forced a chuckle. "Not too much, sadly," she replied evasively. "I've just finished finals, so everything's been crunch time for the last several weeks."

"But you're done for the semester now, right?" Piper chimed in. "Now you can hang out with us more often!"

"Yeah!" Lenore smiled, and the rest of the group went back to talking about trite pleasures while largely ignoring her. It honestly did not trouble Lenore too terribly; if not for John, she would not waste her time with the others. She did her best to be friendly with them, even enthusiastic about their endeavors, but deep down she knew that she would never fully fit in with them because she was the only one of the lot who had any sense of adult responsibility. While everyone else was using their part-time jobs to earn spending money and relying on older family members to pay for necessities, Lenore was using her college grant disbursement to help her mother make up for the difference in rent that the welfare check and her estranged brother's assistance would not cover. Granted, she had always put aside a little money for unnecessary sundries like makeup, as she was clever enough to realize that if she was ever going to rise above repeating the cycle of poverty she was born into, she would have to fake it until she made it. Incidentally, the trick had successfully fooled many people who would otherwise have shunned her out of prejudice, including the fair-weather friends she had at that moment. Only John was aware of her situation, and he himself had darker issues than he let on.

They finally arrived at The Edge of Heaven around fifteen minutes to nine. Lenore slid out of the passenger's seat and smoothed down her outfit, which consisted of a midriff-baring green mock turtleneck, black miniskirt, and gray pantyhose. The backseat group shuffled out of their cramped conditions to reveal their own attire: Matt was dressed in black jeans and a T-shirt of some cartoon character Lenore was not familiar with, Piper wore a low-cut white halter top and tight black yoga pants that flattered her voluptuous tan figure, James kept his pleasantly round torso obscured with a plain black T-shirt and red plaid overshirt, and Alicia maintained a low-key style with an oversized sports jersey and blue jeans. Lenore felt a subconscious tinge of embarrassment at being clearly over-dressed for the occasion, but everyone was familiar enough with her sense of style at that point that they did not think it strange. She followed John across the parking lot toward the entrance of the nightclub, and the others followed behind her.

The crowd inside The Edge of Heaven was thick, but there was still enough room for the group to maneuver toward the bar at the back. Lenore had never been much of an alcohol fan, having had her first and last drink of that nature at seventeen, but given her self-consciousness with John's group, she decided that alcohol might relax her and make her feel more social. She ordered a whiskey and cola, same as the men, while the remaining women opted for more flamboyant drinks. Piper decided to try a dirty martini for the first time, which she immediately regretted. "This tastes like a dirty ass," she lamented, while James and Matt teased her for presuming to know how one would taste.

John, Alicia, and Lenore went to the lounge in the corner of the bar while the others made their way to the dance floor. Through the din of the crowd, Lenore could make out the sound of a George Michael song playing and tapped her foot to the beat as she sipped on her drink. John and Alicia were having a conversation about cars until the former noticed Lenore's subconscious rhythm and put a hand gingerly on her shoulder. "You should go out and dance," he encouraged with a smile.

"I don't know," Lenore chirped, "I don't think I've had quite enough alcohol yet..."

John laughed. "Go on, sweetie. Nobody's judging you."

Lenore looked over at Alicia with a tipsy grin. "What about you, hon? Aren't you gonna dance?"

"Oh no, not me." Alicia waved her hands in dismissal. "I don't dance."

"Well, I wouldn't call myself a great dancer..."

Meanwhile, Piper was nursing her third cocktail as Matt was making small talk and stupid jokes with other patrons in the club. James had somehow been lured into being his wingman, and he seemed almost relieved when Lenore finally decided to mingle with the other half of the group. "Hey Lenore, good to see you," he greeted with his glass raised.

"Hey James. What's up over here?"

"Matt's trying to pick up chicks again."

"Ah. Well, I wish him luck." Lenore glanced over in the general direction of where she had left John and Alicia behind, but a new section of the crowd had already taken advantage of the vacant floor space and blocked viewing access to the lounge. Matt soon rejoined her and James, and after ten minutes of mindless chatter John and Alicia met up with the other three on their own.

John glanced around the bar. "Anyone seen Piper?"

Matt shrugged. "I thought she was with you guys."

James suddenly became very somber, as though he was aware of something the others were not. "She's probably back at the bar."

The group pushed their way through the crowd to find Piper exactly where James expected her to be, sitting and nursing an empty cocktail glass. She turned around slowly, revealing a grave expression and breathlessly creaked, "I don't feel so good."

"Shit," James mumbled, "how much did you drink?"

"I...I don't know," Piper whispered, tears leaking out of her eyes. "I don't feel good…" She attempted to stand up but instead stumbled forward. Matt and James caught her before she fell over completely, and her breasts nearly popped out of her top. The two men grappled to help her stand up straight. "Wh-Where's John? I want John!"

John stepped forward, and she reached out to hug him. Lenore was a little concerned with how comfortable Piper seemed with her male companions, seeing as how she was supposedly in a relationship with someone, but any hint of jealousy went out the window when Piper began dry heaving.

"I'll go call for help," Alicia volunteered, and immediately disappeared from view.

Piper fell out of consciousness before she could vomit, but the remaining four worked to prop her into a sitting position on the floor. The bartender, a skinny blond man in a green apron, glanced over to see if he could be of assistance.

"It's all right." John waved the bartender away. "She's just had a bit too much to drink."

"It's my fault," James muttered. "I should have been keeping an eye on her."

"She's a grown woman," Matt argued. "She should be responsible for herself."

"But she's been having problems with what's-his-name…I'm not going to get into it right now, but she's been confiding in me, and I know she's been depressed…"

"What are we going to do? We can't let Archer know about this, then."

"Alicia's probably going to call her aunt to come get her. She knows what's going on."

Piper started making a gagging noise again. Instead of vomiting, though, she coughed and gasped, "I gotta pee!"

Lenore saw her predicament as both an opportunity to prove her loyalty to these newfound friends and to make herself useful. "I'll take her to the bathroom."

Matt carefully handed Piper off to Lenore. "Are you sure you've got her?"

"Yeah," Lenore assured him. "Which way?"

"That way." Matt pointed to a sign bearing the universal restroom symbols that was located toward one of the back exits of the nightclub.

Lenore did her best to support Piper as she guided the drunk girl toward the ladies' room. "Don't worry, I gotcha…" No one in the crowd offered to help the two women, or even noticed their existence, but they moved out of the way just enough for Piper and Lenore to pass through.

They came to an empty hall with only a drinking fountain on one side and two restroom doors, separated by a crude wooden bench between them. Fortunately, the women's restroom was closer, and Lenore eased Piper into the room, which was no easy task considering the heaviness of Piper's full figure against Lenore's petite frame.

Once inside the dimly-lit, two-stall restroom, Lenore had to help guide Piper onto the toilet. Once Piper was situated on the porcelain throne, Lenore stepped out and closed the stall door behind her. As Piper let out a long, steady stream of urine, Alicia came into the restroom.

"Is she all right?" Alicia asked.

"She's using the toilet right now," Lenore responded. "She hasn't thrown up yet."

"It'll be good for her to throw up." Alicia reached out toward Piper's stall. "Here...I'll take over from here."

"You sure?"

"Yeah, you've already been a huge help. Thank you for this."

"No problem. She'd have done the same for me." Lenore did not know that for certain, but it seemed to be the appropriate thing to say given the scenario. "I'll wait outside in case you guys need me again."

Lenore was worried about Piper, though ultimately was more relived to have a break from the awkward situation. She took a seat at one end of the bench outside, where a tall, husky man in a purple sweatshirt was sitting at the opposite end. He had short brown hair and dark eyes, the same color as Lenore's, and pale skin that suggested he did not often venture outdoors. Lenore wondered what such a person was doing at The Edge of Heaven, since he clearly did not seem the type to frequent nightclubs. She smiled nervously at him and tried to keep to herself, but much to her surprise, the man spoke to her. "Is everything okay?"

"I think so," Lenore replied quietly.

"Your friend just have one too many?"

"Yeah, looks that way. I'm kind of out of the loop, to be honest." She did not know why she felt compelled to give the stranger that information, but it felt refreshing to tell the truth about her insecurity.

"I'm sure she has her reasons," the purple sweatshirt man assured Lenore, and she smiled. "All you can really do is be there for her. I don't necessarily approve of all my friends' choices, but I do my best to be a source of support for them if they need it."

"I guess that's all I can do." Lenore shrugged. "I just wish I could do more."

The purple sweatshirt man smiled. "You know, the Bible has a verse about how the greatest form of love is the willingness to die for one's friends."

*Oh great,* thought Lenore, *an evangelist.* She feared a conversion attempt, so she tactfully attempted to shut him down. "I believe in a higher power, but I don't really subscribe to any religion."

"I know what you mean. I'm kind of the same." Lenore was surprised by his revelation, and she let her guard down a little. The purple sweatshirt man continued, "I think we all have to find our own way to God. Or maybe, he finds us…I don't know, what you think?"

Lenore was not used to being asked for her opinion, and thus was taken aback. "Me? Jeez…I don't know. I never thought about it." She paused, but the purple sweatshirt man made no attempt to interrupt her. "Well…I was raised Christian, whatever that means…but I don't really feel like I was meant for that lifestyle, you know? I mean, I don't even know all the rules, I just know I don't belong there. I'm not really sure I belong anywhere."

"What do you mean?"

"I just feel like I've never been able to live up to anyone's standards. I'm too curious—I expect answers, but I never get them. And I never know what people's motives are."

The man sighed. "I know exactly what you mean."

Lenore began to feel more at ease with the stranger. "If you don't mind me asking…what exactly brought you here tonight?"

"Fate, I guess." He shrugged. "But the long answer…I just came here with a friend. I kind of do odd jobs for his family, and sometimes I keep him out of trouble. But this scene isn't really my thing." He looked at Lenore. "I take it you don't really want to be here, either."

"How'd you guess that?"

"I saw you walk in with your posse a while ago. You didn't seem too enthusiastic."

"Well, they're more my boyfriend's friends than mine…" She felt slightly regretful for mentioning her relationship status, but she was unsure why.

"Does your boyfriend know how you feel?"

"I've never mentioned anything to him…to be honest, I'm not even sure if we're a good match. We don't seem to want the same things…but I should just be grateful anybody wants me, what with my baggage and all…"

He shook his head. "It's not wrong to want to be happy…but if things were different, what kind of man would you be looking for?"

"Well…" Lenore looked down at her hands in her lap, fidgeting with her fingers. "To be honest, most of my fantasies involve me being alone…maybe enjoying the view of a nighttime skyline while listening to Grover Washington, Jr.'s 'Winelight' or something like that. But as for relationships…I'm not into all that social bureaucracy, like what our wedding is gonna be like or how we look as a couple to other people. I just want a guy I can sit at the edge of the universe with, you know?" She could feel her face heating up.

"You mean, like a soul mate?"

"I don't know what you'd call it. I just want a pure love, living in the moment without all the bullshit, like whether or not he's gonna fill all the established roles of a husband, or whether we make a cute couple, or having to choose between a good parent and a good partner…I mean, I get that it's important, but it seems like there always has to be some sort of shallow criteria for a relationship. Or maybe I'm just not mature enough for one."

"I don't think that's unreasonable at all." The man shifted in his spot and readjusted his sweatshirt. "That's pretty much how I feel about relationships. I don't expect to ever find a woman that's my perfect counterpart, but then again, it's just as well…maybe it's better if I focus on myself."

Lenore was a little surprised by his inclination toward heterosexuality, given the color of his sweatshirt and the fact that he had not attempted to be forward with her. She said nothing to that effect, of course. "I know I should do that for myself, but I get so lonely."

He smiled. "Who knows what you can accomplish if you start with yourself?"

Normally, Lenore would have argued a more cynical perspective, but somehow talking to that man gave her some type of hope for the future. She returned his smile. "I guess it's not too late to start over. I mean, I'm only twenty-two, after all."

"Nice…so am I."

They sat in silence for a moment, or as much silence as one could expect to find in a busy nightclub. Finally, the purple sweatshirt man slowly rose to his feet. "I need to step out for some fresh air. You're welcome to join me if you like."

Lenore stood up as well, smoothing her skirt. "Okay."

They walked side-by-side down the hall, out toward the suddenly massive crowd that had formed over the dance floor. As they headed in the general direction of the main exit, a David Bowie tune came blaring over the speaker system, sending everyone into a frenzy to find a dance partner. A wave of eager club patrons in brightly colored attire poured between Lenore and the mysterious man in the purple sweatshirt, separating them like a gushing sea of neon. Lenore could have sworn that she saw the man reach out for her, and perhaps she even reached out for him…

A brown hand clapped Lenore on the shoulder, causing her to jump. She turned around to find John standing behind her. "There you are!" he exclaimed. "Piper's aunt is here. We're ready to go!"

Lenore took one last look across the area where the purple sweatshirt man had been pulled into the human riptide, but he was completely out of sight. Reluctantly, she took John's hand and followed him through the mob, back to where Matt and James were anxiously waiting around. Not long after, they were met by Alicia and Piper, the latter overcoming a sobbing fit, and shoved their way out of the nightclub.

Once outside, they met up with a dirty blue minivan, where a stocky, middle-aged Mexican woman in green nurse's scrubs hopped out of the driver's seat. "Ana Maria!" she cried, racing towards the broken mess that was Piper. Lenore was unsure if the woman was taking an oath for a saint or calling Piper by her Christian name. After easing Piper into the middle seat of the van, the woman turned to glare at the remaining group. "How could you let this happen to her?" she demanded, casting her cold gaze in what Lenore could swear was her direction.

Lenore wanted to state indignantly that if not for her intervention, Piper would have most likely been date raped or dead from alcohol poisoning on the filthy floor of The Edge of Heaven, but she was far too intimidated by the woman's anger to say anything. Fortunately, Matt spoke up instead. "Piper's an adult," he insisted matter-of-factly. "It's not our responsibility to babysit her. That said, we made damn sure that the situation didn't escalate. I suggest taking her to urgent care."

The woman did not seem interested in hearing the group's excuses, but she did not want to waste time arguing with them, either. "We're going home," she said curtly, then stated as an afterthought, "Thank you for taking care of her."

"Let me go with you," Alicia offered. "I'll help her get into some comfortable clothes."

"I'll go, too," James volunteered. "It was my fault she got this bad."

"All right," the woman sighed as she climbed back into the driver's seat. "Get in. We'll talk about this when we get home."

As Alicia and James climbed into the van, Matt suddenly decided to join them. "You go ahead and take Lenore home," he said to John. "Don't worry, she'll be all right." Matt hopped into the van and the woman began driving away before he had even closed the sliding door completely. Once the van had vanished from the parking lot, John put his arm around Lenore's waist.

"Do you think she'll be okay?" Lenore asked.

"I think so," John replied without looking at Lenore. "I know she's been dealing with some shit with her boyfriend, Archer…he's been ignoring her a lot, and she doesn't want to be taken for granted, but they've also been together for two years…"

"Wow, that's pretty rough." Lenore could not think of anything comforting to say, but she did feel bad for Piper's predicament.

"Yeah." John used his free hand to pull a lighter and a pack of cigarettes out of his pocket. "I've tried to offer her advice, but I don't know what to say to her. I'm not very good with relationships myself." He fumbled with his lighter as he lit his cigarette. "To be honest, you're the best girlfriend I've ever had."

Lenore's mood lightened a little. "You mean that?"

"Yeah babe, of course." He inhaled deeply and exhaled a thick cloud of toxic smoke. "My last girlfriend was insane. She was always suspicious of me, and she got her brothers to try and vandalize my car in the middle of the night one time. I don't know what or who the hell she's doing now…"

"She vandalized your car? Did you go to the police?"

"I didn't bother. They wouldn't have done anything."

"Oh." Lenore felt a chill and rubbed her arms. In spite of living in Southern California, where the weather was generally warm year-round, the December nights tended to leave Lenore cold and depressed. While John puffed away at his cigarette, she thought about the man in the purple sweatshirt and wondered if she would ever see him again. She had left her own sweatshirt in John's Mustang, and she wished he would finish his cigarette and take her home, or better yet, take her to bed.

Lenore's frustration was far from merely psychological; she and John had been intimate only six times at that point in their steady partnership, and not one of those times had resulted in a climax for either party. Of course, there was far more to a relationship than sex, which Lenore often had to remind herself, but she was still a woman and she did want to feel loved every once in a while. She stared blindly out into the night, silently berating herself for judging John's abilities as a lover and a boyfriend. *I'm lucky to have someone like John think that I'm special.*

At last, John dropped his cigarette butt on the ground and snuffed it out with the toe of his shoe. "Okay babe," he said, "Let's go." He walked calmly back to his car, and Lenore followed suit.

# CHAPTER TWO

John kept a steady speed on the freeway while Lenore gazed wistfully through the passenger's window. It was well past eleven in the evening and, after the events at The Edge of Heaven, she was ready to retire to a flat sleeping surface and a series of soft blankets. She watched John shift gears as they approached their off-ramp, then went back to watching her surroundings, which consisted of a Denny's chain diner on the corner opposite the off-ramp and an unclaimed area closed off by a chain-link fence.

"Watch this." John nudged Lenore. When she turned to look at him, he shifted the clutch and the black Mustang tore down the street, throwing them both backwards into their seats.

"Whoa!" Lenore gave a surprised laugh as the speedometer climbed higher, first to sixty miles per hour, then eighty. John gradually slowed down when the speedometer hit ninety miles per hour, but once he reached the legal speed limit the car slowed to a crawl, then stopped altogether.

"Damn it!" John attempted to restart the car several times, to no avail.

"Now what?" Lenore asked.

"I can't call the tow guy. My grandpa's the one who pays insurance on this thing, and I've already had it towed twice this month…" John sat pensively for a minute, going over his options internally. "Wait, I have an idea." He unfastened his seat belt, opened his door, and slid out. He then motioned for Lenore to take his place in the driver's seat.

"What can I do?" she protested.

"We're not that far from my place, and we're on top of a slope. We can push it down the block, then I can deal with it in the morning. All I need you to do is guide it with the steering wheel."

Lenore was not overly experienced with automobiles the way John was, but she knew she could manage the steering wheel without difficulty. She took off her seat belt and moved into John's seat, closing the driver's door beside her.

John positioned himself behind the car. "When I give the signal, be prepared to steady the wheel."

"Got it."

With a great deal of effort, they coaxed the dead Mustang down the small hill and onto the street perpendicular to John's cul-de-sac. As Lenore exited the car, she noticed that the full moon was a vibrant red, unlike any harvest moon she had seen before. It stood out against the blue-black sky and the blanket of cool shadows cast upon the cluster of single-story homes that lined the cul-de-sac and adjacent streets. Even as skeptical as she was by nature, she could not help but wonder if it was some type of sign. *Maybe the aliens have finally come for us,* she thought.

After John took the final steps to secure the vehicle and make sure nothing of value was stashed away inside, they grabbed their respective sweatshirts and walked to his house at the end of the cul-de-sac. Since John was not allowed to have company spend the night, he had to wait for his grandfather to fall asleep before sneaking Lenore in through the back door. "Wait here," he whispered, leaving her in the driveway and going inside. The lights were on in the living room, but it was likely to be his older sister in there.

Lenore shuddered. She had met his sister on a few occasions. The girl was always indifferent to her presence, as though she did not expect Lenore to be around for very long. Besides the apparent standoffishness, the girl made Lenore uncomfortable in other ways: she pranced around the house in street clothing that left little more to the imagination than proper underwear, she seemed to have no other purpose in life than to lounge at home and decorate herself, and she bore no physical resemblance to John, not even in ethnicity. Lenore was beginning to suspect that she was not actually John's sister at all, but rather a live-in prostitute that John's grandfather had contracted to help pay for their household's excess. How else would a retired old man and a jobless twentysomething be able to afford expensive cars and prime real estate? Lenore shook her head. *My imagination is running away with me again.*

John came back outside about fifteen minutes later, walking dejectedly down the driveway. "He's still up. He and my sister are going at it again…apparently he smelled weed coming out of her bedroom."

"That's not good."

"And now he's mad at me because of the car, even though this time it wasn't my fault…"

"What are you going to do now?" Lenore was more curious for her own sake, since the buses were no longer running and she would not have the luxury of going home until morning.

"Come with me." He smiled and took her hand. "We'll have some fun."

Together they walked to the nearby liquor store, where John bought a tall bottle of beer and a new pack of cigarettes. While digging around in his wallet for his driver's license at the cashier's station, Lenore entertained herself by identifying all the brands of snack food that were not available in her area. She counted Valley View chips, Holder pretzels, and Westchester toffee before John alerted her to his completion. She then followed him out of the store and back up the street.

They took their goodies up to the small park behind John's cul-de-sac, which was entirely deserted given the time of night. John led Lenore to the park's public restroom, carefully locked up to deter transients from seeking refuge in the stalls, and surprised her when he pulled out a large bronze key to unlock the door. "I'm in good with the maintenance guy here," John explained. "Sometimes I come here to get away from my gramps when the heat is on."

Once inside, John took off his sweatshirt and laid it on the cold cement floor to designate a sitting spot near the wall. They sat down, and John opened the beer with a bottle opener on his keychain. He offered some to Lenore, but she politely declined. "I don't want to be hung over on the bus ride tomorrow morning."

John took a swig from the bottle. "It'll take more than one beer to give me a hangover."

Lenore cuddled closer to John, and he put his arm around her. "I'm glad I have you," he sighed. "You're the only person I can talk to about what's really going on."

"I'm glad I can be here for you." She gave him a gentle squeeze. "What's going on?"

"Just all the shit at home…my grandpa's having heart problems, and my sister might be getting into drugs again…" He took another drink. "Everything's gone to hell since my grandma died. She was the only one who really believed in me, and I'm still struggling to live without her."

"I believe in you," Lenore assured him, but he was too lost in his head to take her confidence to heart.

"My grandma never judged me when I screwed up," he continued. "I know I didn't always make her proud, but she really thought I could do better. Now I'm not sure that I can."

Unsure of what to say, Lenore just gave John a gentle peck on the cheek. He smiled and pulled her closer. She knew that sex was out of the question at that point, but she was not bothered by it—in fact, she felt guilty for wanting it so much while he was suffering emotionally. It was rare for Lenore to encounter a man who did not consider her body a priority in their relationship, and if she had to pick one or the other, she decided that she would opt for the emotional intimacy instead. John continued to lament about the troubles in his life, wondering who he could trust and what he would do with his uncertain future, until both of them drifted off to sleep. It was not a comfortable sleep, as Lenore found herself constantly snapping awake and wondering where she was before dozing off again, but she managed to secure a few hours of uninterrupted slumber before John gently nudged her awake shortly after six in the morning.

"The maintenance guy's gonna be here pretty soon," he whispered. "We should leave."

Lenore groggily sat up and stretched. John seemed eager to usher her along, but she wanted to take a moment to at least rinse the taste of morning breath out of her mouth before catching the bus. She tried turning on each of the faucets on the two sinks—one did not work at all, and the other let out a slow trickle of water that took almost a whole minute to pool up in Lenore's hand. Once she had addressed her minimal hygiene necessity, she followed John out into the breaking dawn.

The streets were ominously quiet. Not a car, not a creature, not a soul could be seen or heard anywhere. The air had settled into a dreamlike stasis; there was no breeze or even the slightest atmospheric change detectable. Lenore chalked it up to the earliness of the hour and her own grogginess, despite having been awake as early before and catching sight of the sure signs of life. Still, she could not shake the feeling that something crucial and bizarre was yet to come, as though she had woken up amid the plot of a David Lynch production.

"I gotta go," John insisted urgently. "I have some family business to attend to. You can make it to the bus stop from here, can't you?"

*Why didn't you mention this before?* Lenore wondered with some annoyance, but replied, "Yeah, I'll be fine."

"All right. I'll see you later."

"When can I see you again?"

"I don't know…I'll call and let you know, okay?" He gave her a quick hug. "I gotta call the mechanic before the busy hour starts."

Lenore thought that John was acting irrationally, but figured he was probably discombobulated from lack of proper sleep.

"Okay. I'll see you later then." Part of Lenore was grateful not to bear witness to John's family drama, but more than that, she cared for her boyfriend and wanted to show her support. *Right now, though, it's best that I leave him to his business and try to get on with my day.*

The bus stop was equally deserted, but the first bus of the day was on schedule. To Lenore's surprise and relief, there were a few people on board—mostly homeless men and one haggard-looking young woman who spoke quietly to herself in schizophrenic ramblings, but people nonetheless. It was difficult to stay awake on the ride home, but somehow she managed to stay vigilant enough to exit at the appropriate stop and return to her mother's apartment. It was a cramped little studio arrangement, compounded by her mother's increasing compulsion to stockpile items she insisted on saving for later, but for the time being, it was the only roof over Lenore's head, and she considered it her responsibility to help her mother maintain occupancy of it.

She looked at her cell phone. *Seven o'clock,* she observed. *Pretty good timing.* "I'm back," Lenore called to her unseen mother as she stepped through the door.

"Hello," her mother called back from the kitchen.

"Sorry I didn't call. There was an incident with one of the girls we were hanging out with, but she's doing better now."

"I sure hope she's okay. What happened?"

"She got a little too drunk."

"Oh." Lenore's mother seemed disappointed that her daughter was associating with alcohol drinkers, despite all of them being of the legal age to consume the substance.

"Like I said, though, she should be all right now." Lenore did not like having to justify her actions as a normal, functioning adult to her mother as though she was a naïve teenager trying to be popular. She made an effort to steer the conversation in a new direction. "Do we still have any of those toaster pastries with the do-it-yourself frosting?"

"You should be careful around these people," Lenore's mother warned.

"They're no threat," Lenore insisted, slightly irritated.

"Don't be a smart ass," called a man's voice from the bathroom. "We're only looking out for your best interest, Lenore."

Lenore froze. "Armin's here?" she asked her mother.

"He's trying to get a job that's closer," her mother explained.

*Shit,* Lenore thought. Armin was not a bad person, per se, but her older brother had a way of being verbally scathing to the point where his words sometimes coerced Lenore into subconsciously feeling guilty or obligated to please him, and by extension, their mother. She heard the toilet flush and the water running, and before she could gather her bearings, Armin stepped out of the bathroom.

"We just don't want you to get all hung up over some guy you put out for, then decide he's not what you want and move on to some other mark like you always do." He zipped his fly for effect. "Also, I ate the last of those toaster pastries, but Mom's gonna get more next month when there's money on the food card again."

"Things are actually going pretty well between me and John." Lenore knew it was futile to try and defend her honor against Armin, but if her mother would not go to bat for her, she had to stick up for herself.

"Sure, Lenore, you say that now…" He brushed by Lenore menacingly while crossing the room to sit in front of the television. "Go take a shower. You reek of cum."

The following month was tense for Lenore, to say the least. She spent most of her free time at the library, losing her conscious mind to a world of fantasy books, or texting acquaintances on the inexpensive cell phone she had paid for with a portion of her grant disbursement. For the most part, Armin left her to her own devices, but he noticed that Lenore's correspondence with John was waning and decided to call her out on it.

"He's been busy with family drama," Lenore insisted, though she herself thought it strange that he was becoming increasingly unavailable. The last time she had heard from him was on New Year's Eve, when she had come down with a cold and John counted down to 2013 with her over the phone. He insisted that he was not doing anything special to celebrate, save for maybe throwing back a few beers with friends, but Lenore distinctly heard a large crowd ushering in the new year in the background. Then again, perhaps his sister had some of her friends over, or maybe even extended family. She did not want to be the one to constantly keep tabs on her boyfriend, but she certainly did not want to lose him, though Lenore was unsure whether it was a sign of love or another subconscious longing to not let her family down with another failed relationship.

The second week of January went by with only sparse texts from John. Lenore thought it was highly inappropriate for an established couple to go for such a length of time with such minimal contact, barring excruciating circumstances, but only when John's messages ceased entirely did she decide to make the matter known among their circle. She chose to text Alicia first, since Alicia had known John the longest out of all of them.

*Hey, have you seen or heard from John lately?*

It took about half an hour for Alicia to text back, *No, he's been busy.*

Lenore decided to wait another day before texting another friend, lest she come across as some sort of obsessive control freak.

*Hey Matt, have you heard from John lately?*

Matt responded almost immediately with *No, stop asking about him.*

At that moment, Lenore knew she was being deceived. She picked up her cell phone and dialed John's number, prefixed with a number blocker to prevent the caller ID from giving her away. It was a long shot, since most people she knew did not answer incoming calls from unknown sources, but she managed to make a connection.

"Hello?" a female voice picked up the phone.

"Hello, is John here?" Lenore asked innocently.

There was a faint smacking on the other end of the line, like the chewing of gum. Lenore realized she must be talking to John's sister, as she was presumably the only person outside of a 1990s situation comedy to think that abusing such a habit over the phone was acceptable. "Just a sec. Who is this?"

"This is Lenore."

"Lenore who?"

"Lenore Kavaranian."

"Okay. One sec, Lenore." There was a brief pause, silent save for the sticky static of her gum chewing, before John's sister responded. "Nope, he's not here right now."

*This bimbo takes me for a fool,* Lenore seethed internally. *Why in the blue hell would he leave his cell phone behind, much less permit his sister to take calls that could just as easily go to voicemail?* "Okay, thanks. Can you let him know I called?"

"Sure thing. Have a blessed day!"

Lenore distinctly heard John's sister whisper "So you're not seeing her?" before the connection was cut.

The next day, Lenore woke up early to take the bus to John's house, with the intent of paying him a surprise visit to catch him off-guard. She carefully applied her makeup and wore her favorite slim black jeans, for added confidence, along with a T-shirt featuring a Japanese-inspired candy motif and the phrase "Sugar Land" illustrated on the front. Donning her black commander's cap and sweatshirt to complete the ensemble, she was ready to face whatever lay ahead. Careful not to wake Armin, who was sleeping strategically on the floor by the exit, she said goodbye to her mother and quietly left.

The bus ride to John's house was always long, as he lived on the other side of the city, but that time the commute felt like the blink of an eye, leaving Lenore little time to prepare psychologically for her confrontation. She tentatively walked to John's cul-de-sac and risked a glance down the dead-end street. John's Mustang was missing, but it may have been in the body shop, for all Lenore knew. A cherry-red Toyota was parked neatly at the end of the cul-de-sac, which Lenore recognized as belonging to John's grandfather, but she did not want to risk another incident like her encounter over the phone with John's sister. Disappointed and frustrated, she decided to pass the time by walking to the nearest liquor store, buying a soft drink and then walking back toward John's street to see if anything had changed. Once she saw that everything was how she left it, she continued walking until she found a

16

park bench that gave her a clear view of the street perpendicular to the cul-de-sac. That way, she could see any vehicle turning into it and act accordingly.

An hour into her stakeout, Lenore saw the most unusual butterfly she had ever happened upon: a large yellow insect with black stripes, lined with a strip of black around the edges of its wings. It fluttered about in a haphazard trajectory, threatening more than once to crash into Lenore's head. Although terrifying when flying close to her face, Lenore found the creature fascinating and followed it around the park until it disappeared into a linden tree, prompting her to look down the street just as a large white car was turning into the cul-de-sac. *Matt's car.*

Taking that as her cue to investigate, Lenore strode down the street with purpose. Sure enough, Matt had parallel parked at the end of the cul-de-sac. Piper, James, and Alicia followed him up the path to John's front door. Lenore arrived at the edge of the driveway just as John opened the door to greet his friends. When he saw Lenore appear behind the group, his expression grew sober.

"What the hell is she doing here?" John demanded, prompting the others to turn around.

Lenore felt more intimidated with the entire group there to bear witness to what she had to say, but she had already written them off as fair-weather acquaintances and knew they would take John's side, no matter what grievous sin he had committed. She stared past them and locked eyes with John. "I'm not here to bother you," she insisted, "I just want answers. I know I'm not a great person, but I think I'm owed at least a little respect, considering I *thought* I was your steady girlfriend for the past five months."

"I'm done with you," John growled.

"Can I at least know why?"

"Because…look at this. You're clingy as hell, and depressing."

That struck a nerve with Lenore. "Clingy? What have I done that's clingy? Care about you? Like when you cried like a little bitch that I was the only one who showed up to your twenty-second birthday party?"

"Hey, I was there!" Alicia interrupted. "You leave him alone!"

"Yeah, but not before making some bullshit excuse as to why you couldn't make it at first. I don't think any of you guys would be friends if you guys didn't have money to go drinking and eating out all the time. God forbid any of you should have to pay an electric bill, or buy groceries with actual money…" She turned her attention to Matt. "And Matt, you unfunny try-hard, just because you hang out with a bunch of Mexicans doesn't mean that you're going to get white girls to choose you out of the group by default." Lenore turned back to John. "I don't know what ass-backwards morals your real parents raised you with, but when *normal* people want to end a relationship, they don't just ignore someone until they go away. Get back to third grade with that shit."

"What makes you think I ever *wanted* to be in a relationship with you?" John was clearly grasping at straws, but Lenore was too angry to take advantage of his weakness.

"That high-class call girl you try to pass off as a sister seemed to think we were an item. Maybe she's the one you left me for. I don't know, I'm done caring. I'll see you all in hell." Lenore turned to leave, but Piper grabbed her.

"Where do you think you're going, bitch?" she yelled. "You don't just come in here and talk trash to me and my friends like that."

Lenore smiled. "It's nice to see your confidence is back, Piper. Maybe if you used some of that to talk to your boyfriend, you wouldn't have to drink yourself into a coma every night. You're welcome for helping you not piss all over yourself, by the way."

Lenore braced herself for a punch in the face, but instead, Piper crumpled to the ground in tears. While everyone else tripped over themselves to console her, Lenore took the opportunity to make her getaway.

She ran toward the bus stop, and by the grace of God, was somehow able to make it just in time to catch the bus back home. Out of breath and coming to terms with what had happened, Lenore let her own tears fall as the bus pulled her safely away from yet another ex-boyfriend and his disproportionate number of allies. Once again, she was alone.

# CHAPTER THREE

The spring semester at Lenore's community college started three days after the incident with John DeLuna and company, which gave Lenore a welcome excuse for not being at home. Besides wanting to avoid Armin, she sought to keep a low profile in case her new enemies came to bother her. Fortunately, they seemed to have no further interest in tormenting Lenore, so she was able to devote the bulk of her stress onto school and financial matters.

Her first grant disbursement would not be available until the second week of the semester, but Lenore's professor for Advanced Algebra was not only one of the rare college instructors who required the assigned textbook, but a stringent authoritarian who expected the students to have said textbook on the very first day of class. Even if Lenore had her money in hand on that very day, the campus bookstore had been recently depleted by hordes of naïve students desperate to secure the required reading at a ninety percent markup, unaware that they would only be able to trade in the books at the end of the term for a mere decimal percentage of its worth, if at all. Until she had her disbursement and could order a cheaper copy online, she would have to screw up her courage and ask a colleague if she could borrow their book in the meantime.

Most of the students seemed unapproachable, having formed their own circles and cliques out of preservation for their social brand. Lenore had no friends at the community college, preferring to focus on obtaining her degree without distraction, although she had managed to find that elsewhere. However, being in her penultimate semester before graduation, it was pointless to try cutting into existing groups. Nevertheless, she needed an Algebra textbook, and she needed someone to take pity on her predicament.

As soon as the professor released his class for the day, Lenore merged with the exodus of students, staking out a possible study partner. It was nigh impossible to figure out who had a textbook that way, especially since most of the group was already texting away on their cell phones or rushing off to other classes. Since that was the only class Lenore had scheduled until later in the week, she decided to use up her free time by reading a novel in her favorite secluded spot on campus.

There was a section of the Humanities wing with a clearing, the center of which was a raised architectural island with a large tree. Lenore liked to sit under that tree and read or do homework, or even rest on a sunny day. She made her way over to her spot, only to find a stubby young man with a loose mop of strawberry blond curls sitting there, doing his homework. By the time Lenore saw him there she was already too close, and he made eye contact with her before she could humbly back away. She opened her mouth to apologize for the awkward encounter, and then realized that he had a copy of the Advanced Algebra textbook she needed.

"Did you just get out of that class?" Lenore inquired, pointing to the book.

"Yeah," he replied.

"Would you mind if I copied the problems out of your book? I'm waiting on my disbursement before I can get my own."

The young man shifted over, giving Lenore space to sit next to him. "Sure, go ahead."

"Thanks, you're a lifesaver." Lenore sat down in the spot he made for her. "I'm Lenore, by the way."

"Seth." He stuck out his hand and Lenore shook it. "I'm new to this campus. I've only got a few more credits to get, though. Then I'm out of here."

"My next semester will be my last, God willing."

"Well, good luck with that."

"Thanks, you too." Lenore smiled and took out her pencil and spiral-bound notebook. Seth set the textbook between them so they could use it simultaneously, and together they worked on their first Advanced Algebra assignment.

They met twice a week—after each class meeting—to use the book together. Seth was more well-versed in arithmetic than Lenore was, although not quite adept at explaining things in the simplest of terms, but she still benefited from his academic influence. Although Lenore's grant disbursement came in at the end of the second week, Seth told her she could continue using his book to do her homework.

"At least let me pay you half of what the book cost," Lenore insisted.

"Don't worry about it." Seth waved his arm in dismissal. "My mom paid for my school books, anyway."

They then decided to exchange phone numbers, just in case they had any questions about the assignment or one of them would be absent. Lenore texted Seth later that night just to make sure she had the right number programmed into her phone. He confirmed his number, then engaged her in casual conversation.

*How's the homework coming?* he asked.

*I finished it while I was waiting for the bus,* Lenore replied.

*Nice. I'm still working on mine.*

*Good luck with that.*

*Thanks, I'll need it.*

Lenore felt the corners of her mouth turn up into a smile. It had been a long time since she had felt at ease talking to another human being.

The next time Seth and Lenore met up, Seth pulled out a small storage container full of chocolate chip cookies. "My mom made these to take for a snack," he explained, "but I can't eat them all in one sitting, and they're only good fresh. Want to help me eat them?"

Lenore was never one to turn down a free meal. "Sure, thanks!" She picked a cookie out of the container and took her usual place next to Seth. He handed her the textbook, and she gently brushed his arm as she moved to receive it. He did not seem to notice, or at least was not bothered by it, but Lenore became slightly flustered by the accidental touch. She turned her attention to the textbook, focusing instead on copying down the problems on the page. When she finished, she handed the book back to Seth, and he gave her the container of cookies instead.

"The rest are yours," he offered. "I'm getting a little too chunky for my liking."

Lenore looked him over. He was a little chubby in the middle, but by no means overweight. If anything, Lenore found his pudgy belly to be rather endearing. She had always preferred her men to have a bit of weight on them, and she was ashamed to admit that it had been somewhat awkward to engage in carnal relations with John when his waist was almost the same size as hers. Still, she decided to play it safe with Seth. "You don't look chunky to me."

Seth smiled sardonically. "You're just humoring me…but thanks."

Lenore checked the time on her cell phone. "I should probably head out to the bus stop soon…"

"Okay. Go ahead and take the cookies with you. Just bring back the Tupperware when you're done."

"All right then. I'll see you next week."

"Laters."

As Lenore sat silently on the bus, she found Seth creeping into her thoughts. By that time, it had been well over a month since John had broken up with her, and she no longer missed his companionship. It had been even longer since she had any sort of physical release, and her living arrangements made any sort of self-satisfaction unfeasible, especially with Armin around. Besides the lack of privacy, there was the unspoken stigma of autoerotic activities, most likely a remnant of an upbringing in religious morality. Even then, it was not the climax that Lenore sought after so much as the act itself: the power of being able to provide for a partner in a way no one else could, the comfort of being caressed and adored when she was at her most vulnerable, and the adrenaline rush that made her forget how frustrating her short life had been thus far.

Once Lenore made it safely home, Armin made her wish she had stayed longer. "Oh great, she's back," he grumbled, leaving Lenore to guess at what slander he might have spewed in her absence. Lenore said nothing as she slipped off her shoes and backpack, setting them gently beside her sleeping space before sitting down against a propped-up pillow. She opened her backpack to retrieve her homework, then remembered the container she had brought home with her. Pulling them out of her backpack, she asked, "Anybody want some chocolate chip cookies?"

Armin eyed her suspiciously. "Where'd you get chocolate chip cookies?"

"A friend's mom made them. They're pretty good." She opened the container and held it up for Armin to take one.

Armin looked at her as though he needed inspiration to come up with other insults, but instead reached into the container and accepted her offer. "Thanks."

"No prob." She looked around for her mother. "Where's Mom?"

"She's out getting a money order for the rent note."

Lenore felt a hint of irritation pulse through her right eye. It seemed to Lenore that her mother thought little of her, given her passive acceptance of Armin's mistreatment and subtle expressions of disappointment, yet the old woman had no problem accepting money from her. Furthermore, there was the question of why Lenore's mother was unable to afford the rent on her own in the first place: could she not find a job on her own? Why did she not encourage her children to move out and fend for themselves? Much like Lenore's hands-off exposure to Christianity, she did not have answers for these questions, and thus was dissatisfied with the impact of the unsolved problems in her daily life.

To be fair, Lenore was not entirely blameless for the way she was scrutinized by Armin and her mother. In her younger days, she had been something of a rebel. Perhaps it was another side effect of her discontentment with her mother's explanations, or maybe Lenore herself was born with the fatal flaw of not being able to think critically with only limited information presented. Either way, she had been tragically sure of herself to the chagrin of her family—when her determination saw success, she was met with silent indignation; when her pigheadedness failed, she gained no sympathy. Additionally, she had often been unabashedly outspoken about her intentions, be they the pursuit of pleasure or a goal that others deemed unachievable. She initially meant to create a façade that would protect her from unnecessary shame, but it only succeeded in making those around her uncomfortable. It was only within the last six months or so that Lenore became aware of her unfavorable pattern of actions, and she sought to correct them, but the damage had been done. In spite of her desire to always change for the better, in her family's mind, she had been pigeonholed as "the same old Lenore" from the earliest age at which she had done wrong.

As the weekend fell, Lenore found herself thinking of Seth all the time, all the while denying that she was becoming attracted to him. Finally, she realized, *If I have to keep telling myself I don't have a crush on him, then I probably do.*

Her next meeting with Seth had her feeling a little nervous. She tried to let her mind go blank, filling it instead with the monotony of algebraic equations, but her eyes kept wandering back to him as he sat hunched over under the tree, merely inches away. Objectively, he was average-looking, with his strawberry blond curls and pale, lightly-freckled skin. He was not much taller than Lenore, although John, too had been below average height for a male. Lenore could not tell if his eyes were blue or green, as they could go either way depending on the light source, but she found them to be beautiful. *But he's too decent,* Lenore told herself. *He would never go for someone like me. Besides, I have nothing to offer him.*

Lenore and Seth continued their routine, and as the weeks went by, their relationship became less of an academic convenience and more of a legitimate friendship. They would socialize longer, sometimes watching internet videos on the campus library's computers when they could get away with it, other times walking around campus while shooting the breeze, or even taking a trip down the block to the local shopping plaza for lunch at a fast food restaurant. Had anyone around them bothered to pay them any attention, they would have appeared to be a cute couple discovering their infatuation for one another. At first, Lenore shied away from the darker aspects of her life, but gradually she began to open up about her living situation and her hidden fears that she would never actually do anything with her life.

"I understand how you feel," Seth sympathized. "My mom and I have been struggling for years to get by after my dad died. I'm hoping I'm able to get an engineering job soon after I graduate."

Lenore felt more comfortable after finding out that Seth understood destitution firsthand, but opted to focus on lighter subject matter to keep her time with Seth pleasant. Finally, Seth decided to ask the hard question one day: "So, are you seeing anyone?"

Lenore was caught off-guard by his inquiry. In her mind, there was only one reason why anyone would ask about another's relationship status, especially after having had the opportunity to infer that information beforehand. "Why?"

"Just curious." Seth looked down dejectedly. "I hadn't thought to ask sooner."

"I had a boyfriend about a month ago…right now, I don't expect anyone good to be interested in me."

Seth raised an eyebrow. "Anyone *good?*"

"Yeah, you know…someone who's not a complete piece of crap. Like, there's the industry standard of a guy who's not abusive or a cheater, but I'm talking about a guy with a good head on his shoulders… someone with ambitions and convictions and stuff. Someone I can have an actual relationship with, if that makes sense." Lenore found it easier to explain to Seth what type of relationship partner she wanted rather than her ideal soul mate, as not to unintentionally scare him off.

"Well, that seems logical. What's stopping you from finding a guy like that?"

"None of those types of guys are interested in me," she lamented. "They all want girls from higher-income backgrounds who are virginal and naïve, who they aren't embarrassed to show to their mothers. I'm not like that, and I can't change who I am."

"I'm interested in you." Seth shrugged, as though he was expecting a clear rejection. "Just throwing that out there."

Lenore was surprised, but could not help smiling. "You like *me?* What do you like about *me?*"

"Well, we like doing things together, and we can talk about anything…" He smiled the first genuine smile Lenore had seen in all the time she had known him. "Plus…I think you're really hot." He blushed and quickly directed his gaze to the ground.

"So, you're saying you want to get more serious?" Lenore wanted to make sure she understood him correctly. "But I don't know what you'd want of me in a relationship. I'm still trying to get my shit together."

"Isn't everyone? All I ask for in a relationship is loyalty, affection, companionship…" He took Lenore's hands in his. "Why let a good thing slip away out of fear of not being good enough?"

At last they made eye contact. Lenore's heart was racing and her stomach was becoming increasingly acidic, so she leaned forward to kiss Seth, hoping to break the tension. His lips felt warm and soft against hers, and she relaxed into his arms.

In the weeks to come, they became as secure in their physical expression as they had already become in their emotional bond, culminating the weekend after midterms during an opportunity when Seth's mother was out of town. Lenore had underestimated how much she missed a lover's touch, eagerly straddling Seth as he guided her delicately curved bottom over his uncovered lap until she unexpectedly released her frustration in a moment of vocal ecstasy. Seth was simultaneously shocked and delighted, further enticing him to his own climax. After disposing of the wet latex sheath that had protected their sensibilities during copulation, Seth pulled Lenore beside him and held her close. She returned the embrace and rested her head on his bare chest.

"I needed that," Lenore sighed.

"I'm glad I could make you feel good." Seth kissed the top of Lenore's head. "I'm surprised you came so quickly."

"I'm surprised I came at all. I've never been this comfortable with anyone before..." Lenore moved up slightly to meet Seth's eyes. "I hope you enjoyed it, too."

"Of course I enjoyed it. I hope we get to do it again soon."

"How soon?"

"As soon as possible."

Lenore looked around Seth's apartment. It was larger than the one she shared with Armin and her mother, being a single bedroom unit rather than a studio, but Seth and his mother were not receiving any sort of government assistance, thus their income was likely more strained if they were close to the poverty line. Seth's mother had the bedroom to herself while Seth slept on a futon in the living room, which Lenore thought was oddly selfish of a parent, but it was certainly an arrangement she could empathize with.

Seth sat up and examined his cell phone. "My mom should be back in an hour."

Lenore's heart sank. "How soon should I leave?"

Seth looked confused. "Leave? You don't want to meet her?"

"Oh, she knows about me?" Lenore knew it sounded stupid the second it flew out of her mouth. "I mean, she's okay with me?"

"Well, yeah. I told her you're my girlfriend, and how awesome you are..." Seth fumbled around on the floor for his boxers. "She said I should bring you around sometime."

"Well, I don't have anywhere important to be." Lenore knew she could always call her mother and tell her if she planned to come home late.

Seth and Lenore finished hunting down their missing articles of clothing and put them back on. The two of them then sat on the couch, cuddling and watching DVDs of old 1990s cartoons until the front door creaked open.

"Hey Mom." Seth rose from his seat to greet his mother. "I want you to meet someone."

Seth's mother was taller and slightly thinner than he was, and looked to be in her late forties, though she was likely much older. Lenore flashed an awkward smile at the woman and waved. "Hello."

"You must be Lenore. What a beautiful name." Seth's mother spoke with a level of eloquence that Lenore was not accustomed to. "I'm Marnie."

"Nice to meet you," Lenore greeted.

Marnie turned to Seth. "Is she staying for dinner?"

"I don't know, Mom. I haven't asked her yet." He looked over at Lenore. "Well...do you want to have dinner with us?"

"I'd like to," Lenore replied, "but I have to catch the bus to get back home, and they don't run as late on the weekends."

"Well, I can drop you off," Marnie offered. "Where do you live?"

Lenore's throat went dry. If she accepted Marnie's offer for dinner and the subsequent ride home, Marnie would see that she lived in the underdeveloped part of town. If she declined, she ran the risk of making a bad impression on Marnie, and it was not often that the parent of a romantic partner took an active interest in knowing her better. Lenore felt awkward, but she swallowed her pride and accepted the invitation anyway. After calling her mother and letting her know she would be back later in the evening, the three of them had a nice chicken dinner and watched an old movie. By the end of the evening, Lenore felt right at home.

At a quarter to nine, Marnie suggested they wrap it up. "It was nice getting to know you, Lenore," she said sweetly, although Lenore had not told Marnie anything that Seth had not already informed his mother about.

"You too." Lenore was apprehensive about the ride home, but Marnie seemed unaware that she lived in a bad neighborhood. They said their goodbyes, and Lenore enjoyed the slow walk up to the front door of her mother's apartment as she braced herself for the neurotic scene Armin had likely prepared at her expense.

Sure enough, Armin was watching TV, waiting for his sister to arrive. "You have another roll in the hay already? Seems like only yesterday you were *so in love* with John..."

"I will love whoever I'm with," Lenore replied matter-of-factly. "But yeah, I was spending time with Seth. I got to meet his mom today."

"So, you're going to start spending all your time over there...sounds about right. You might as well move over there. My work can cover the rent, so we don't need you around here."

Lenore glared at her mother, questioning her maternal loyalties with a frigid gaze before turning back to Armin. "I intend to move out with Seth someday."

Armin rolled his eyes. Fortunately, their mother spoke up before he could think of another snide remark. "What did you have for dinner?"

"Fried chicken."

"Deep-fried or oven-fried?"

"Pan-fried, I think. I mean, it was over the stove."

Armin turned his annoyance over to their mother. "How come *we* never have fried chicken?"

"Well," their mother began, and then Lenore tuned out their conversation. For once, she decided to try not to let her family chip away at her happiness. She closed her eyes and silently relived the day's earlier events in her mind. *I hope to God this isn't too good to be true.*

# CHAPTER FOUR

The spring semester ended almost as quickly as it began. Although they no longer shared a class, Lenore and Seth continued to see each other whenever possible, not the least of which was in various states of undress. At some point in the previous term, Lenore had narrowly resisted the temptation to make love to Seth in one of the less-frequented restrooms on campus, and their youthful hormones continued to govern their personal interactions with one another. In addition to strengthening their intimate bond, it served to reduce the strain on their individual lives, be it Lenore's final semester of community college or Seth's fruitless search for an engineering job in the area.

"Once I get a job, I can start saving up so we can move in together," Seth promised Lenore after another passionate session in his mother's absence.

"I would love that," Lenore replied dreamily. "And once I find work, I'll be able to put money toward those savings as well."

"I don't want you to worry about that right now. You just focus on your classes, and do the best you can."

For the first time, Lenore had an idea of exactly what she wanted to do with her life: she was going to set aside whatever money she could spare from her next disbursement and save up to move out of her mother's apartment. She would earn her happiness, and in the process, help Seth attain his. Together they might be able to afford a humble little apartment, then draw motivation from their love for each other to work their way up to the American Dream. She had mentioned it to Seth, who seemed to like the idea, but he still insisted that she focus her mental energy on achieving her degree. "But the fall semester doesn't start until August, and there's still the rest of the summer in the way."

"Well then...let's enjoy the summer."

As luck would have it, the summer was a flash in the pan. Armin kept himself busy doing odd jobs for freelance pay, leaving Lenore alone for the most part. Lenore herself took the opportunity to sort through her belongings and clear out things she no longer needed, but only when her mother was not at home, in order to prevent the old lady from reclaiming antiquated clothes and toys that were meant to be discarded or donated. By the time the fall semester rolled around, Lenore felt like she was becoming a new person.

The fall semester itself swept by largely without incident, save for the occasional deadpan insult from Armin whenever Lenore attempted a social conversation with their mother. Lenore still carved out quality time to spend with Seth, who never grew tired of her and never let a day go by without so much as a "Good morning" text. She was honestly surprised that their relationship had lasted so long, in spite of a latent fear that something would go horribly wrong. Shortly before Thanksgiving, though, Seth broke the constancy with some life-changing news.

Lenore received two missed call notifications from him while she was in class. She knew he would not bother her during those hours if it was not an emergency, so she called him back as soon as the session ended. "What's wrong?" she demanded.

"I couldn't wait to tell you," Seth cried.

"Tell me what?" Lenore braced herself for the worst news possible: Seth was leaving her, he or Marnie was in the hospital, they were suddenly homeless…but Seth was brimming with excitement.

"We got a new apartment!" he exclaimed. "We can move in at the end of December."

*You got me all worked up for this?* Lenore wanted to be excited, but having prepared herself for a verbal apocalypse, she did not know how to feel about the actual news. "So…what's going to happen?"

"Mom and I are moving to a two-bedroom apartment in Citrus. And we want you to come with us."

Lenore was taken aback. "Is…is this a joke?"

"No joke, I swear. I finally got a job out there, so we're moving closer to my work. I'm letting you know now so you have time to pack."

Lenore let out an excited squeal. She could not believe that her dreams were coming true. She was going to live with Seth—albeit with Marnie as well, but she and Seth's mother were quite amicable—and be able to find a job in another city. "I'll start packing at once!"

When Lenore returned home that day, she was impatient for the chance to tell her mother the good news. However, her mother and Armin did not receive the information with quite the same zeal as Lenore had.

"What do you mean you're moving at the end of December?" Armin bellowed. "How are we going to continue making the rent?"

"What are you talking about?" Lenore asked angrily. "You said your job would more than cover what I was paying."

"I haven't had an actual job since last year," Armin fired back. "Why the hell do you think I moved back here?"

Lenore wondered why Armin and her mother found it necessary to hide that crucial bit of information from her, though in retrospect, it became rather obvious. "There's work to be had in Citrus. Seth found a job out there."

"And I take it you're going to find a job and send money back here? You're going to be too busy screwing Seth to pay any attention to us."

"Excuse me? I'm twenty-three years *old.* It's my God-given *right* to move out and start a new life for myself, even a new family. This is what I'm *supposed* to be doing." She directed her gaze at her mother. "And why don't *you* work?"

"I wouldn't be able to make enough to afford this apartment without welfare," her mom explained.

"You don't make enough to afford this place *now!*" Lenore felt a vein pulsing in her temple, and took a deep breath to calm her self. "And if I don't find a job out here, what's the point?"

Lenore's mother let out an audible sigh, the type she was prone to whenever her daughter disappointed her with a misguided sense of independence. "Well, I can't force you to live here."

"Wait, I know." Lenore went to her sleeping spot and pulled out a large pickle jar filled with money. "I don't know how much is in here, but I was saving up to someday get an apartment with Seth. But you guys need it more." She held it up in presentation to her mother.

"We don't need your charity," Armin grumbled, but her mother reached out and took the jar without hesitation. He shot a contemptuous glance at the old woman.

"Thank you," her mother said.

Lenore replied with a customary "You're welcome," but she resented her mother for having the audacity to take money from her without making the slightest attempt at showing her due respect, such as understanding Lenore's needs as a functional adult or defending her against her brother's verbal abuse. *After this,* Lenore vowed, *they're as good as cut off from my life.*

She did manage to save a little money to pay for the moving truck and heavy-duty plastic storage bins that she would organize her belongings in to stave off the destructive insects and spiders that accumulated in the cluttered apartment. She had done most of her weeding out over the summer, which made it easier for her to pack given the limited time span and college schedule. She and Seth had little face-to-face interaction during that time, given the circumstances, but they would always text each other throughout the day and call each other at least once a week in the evening. Once the holidays and the fall semester were finally over, the big day approached.

Marnie had hired professional movers to help her and Seth with their property, but she drove a moving truck out to Lenore's apartment herself. Seth rode shotgun to help out.

"They're here!" Lenore exclaimed. She had already moved all of her bins out to the front of the apartment to save her the embarrassment of having Seth or Marnie see what kind of squalor she had been living in, not to mention the fact that both Armin and her mother had adamantly refused to meet them.

Marnie greeted Lenore from the truck's cab. "It sure would be nice to meet your family," she mused sweetly.

"They're not here right now," Lenore lied. "They had to pick something up at the post office."

"Oh, that's too bad." She shooed Seth out of the cab. "Go on, now. Be a gentleman and help her load her stuff into the back."

Seth came down from his seat to assist Lenore. "It's good that you had the foresight to put your things in plastic tubs," he mentioned.

"Just had to keep the spiders and crap out," Lenore explained evasively. There were only five bins to place in the truck, which were mostly filled with bedding, clothes, and books. When they were finished, Seth and Lenore squeezed into the shotgun seat together next to Marnie.

"No furniture?" Marnie inquired. "Not even a bed?"

"I'm leaving all that with my mom and brother." It was another lie, although there were several old things that Lenore did not bother to take either because they were decrepit or because she thought her mother and brother could use them more.

The ride to Citrus was cramped and long. Lenore spent the whole trip staring blankly out of the passenger's window while Seth and Marnie chatted about a topic she was not privy to, making careful observations about her surroundings. There was a long expanse of flat, uncharted land, marked only by faded purple mountains in the distance. The mountains became more sparse as they journeyed closer to their destination, and soon, buildings began to appear—first small houses and trailer parks, then commercial areas, until finally, they were within the city limits of Citrus, California.

Lenore sat up. "Wow, this place is huge."

Seth chuckled. "It is a bit different from what we're used to, isn't it?"

"Yeah. It's a nice change of pace, really."

"I hate the noise of the city," Marnie lamented. "It gets so busy at night, and you can always hear the car alarms going off at ungodly hours in the morning."

"Hopefully we won't have that problem," Seth chimed in.

"Personally, I'm looking forward to having my own bedroom." He nudged Lenore with his elbow and raised his eyebrows suggestively.

Marnie was oblivious to the innuendo. "Seth hasn't had a room of his own since his father passed and we had to move into the old place," she clarified.

Lenore thought about asking why he was not given the solitary bedroom in the old apartment, as most parents she had known would have done in a similar situation, but she figured there was a logical reason behind it somewhere and let it go. "I know the feeling."

Marnie made a left turn and pulled into a storage center, prompting a jolt of confusion from Lenore. After punching a code into a number pad and triggering the gate open, she parked the truck next to one of the closest units. Seth gave Lenore a gentle push to usher her out of the cab, and the two of them went around to the back of the truck.

"What are we doing here?" Lenore asked.

"The apartment's kind of small," Seth explained, "so we're gonna have to put most of your things in storage for a while. Just keep the tub that has the most important stuff."

"You should have told me this beforehand." Lenore tried her best to keep her temper even. "I have everything scattered around."

"Hmm…why don't you just switch some things around real quick?"

"All right, I'll see what I can do." Lenore lifted the lids on all of her bins and briefly scanned the contents. She picked the tub she found to be most important and threw other necessities into it—tampons, hairbrush, her copy of *Illusions* by Richard Bach, and a black pageboy cap. "This is the one I'll take—the others can go into storage."

"What's taking so long?" Marnie called from the cab.

"Nothing, it's fine," Seth shouted back. He stacked the remaining four bins on top of one another and aggressively shoved them into the storage unit, which was already crowded with unused furniture and cardboard boxes.

"Be careful with my antique dresser!" Marnie yelled at Seth. "I paid good money for that."

Lenore stole a quick glance at the dresser in question—a plain, unfinished, birch-colored wooden dresser covered with dust. *That piece of crap?*

When Seth finished his task, he and Lenore took the bin over to the parking lot, where Marnie's black Toyota RAV4 was parked. "*Now* we're going to our new place. Aren't you excited?"

Lenore perked up. "Yeah!"

Seth kissed Lenore's cheek. "We're going to be together forever!"

After loading the bin in the back and hopping into the RAV4, they drove to the Westchester Apartments, parallel parking on the street outside of the main office. It was a grand series of two-story buildings on a cul-de-sac, each section its own gated community decorated inside and out with a variety of trees and seasonal blooms. The apartments themselves were a light salmon color, highlighted by the strategic placement of decorative tiles of marbled blue, brown, and gray. The three of them exited the vehicle and slowly walked up to the office, the click of their shoes on the concrete echoing into the empty daylight.

A middle-aged woman with wrinkled brown skin in a red pantsuit greeted them as they entered the office. "Hello. Are you looking for rental information?"

"We're new tenants," Marnie corrected. "I'm Marnie Horvitz, and this is my son, Seth." She motioned to Seth, who stepped forward on cue.

"Hello." He managed a vague wave.

The lady in red brought them to a corner of the room with a forest green loveseat, a matching chair, and a cherry wood desk stacked with a computer and heaps of paperwork. Not knowing what else to do, Lenore followed them in a stupor. She sat down on the chair, Marnie and Seth sat on the loveseat, and the office lady took a seat behind the desk.

"I'm Celina," the lady introduced, "and I'll be processing your information." Celina brought her intricately manicured hands up to the keyboard and began clacking away. "Okay. So, you and your son are the new tenants, correct?"

"That's right," Marnie confirmed.

Lenore raised an eyebrow. When Seth told her that he and Marnie found an apartment for all three of them, she assumed that the three of them would be named equally on the lease. *Perhaps this is just the credit information,* she thought.

Celina moved the computer mouse around a few times, ticking boxes here and there. "Okay, any pets?"

"No," Marnie replied.

"Waterbeds?"

"No."

"Any hazardous medical equipment, like oxygen…" Celina's voice faded into obscurity as Lenore tried to distract herself mentally. She sat primly and patiently for forty-five minutes through the final steps of apartment rental bureaucracy, taking in all the important details regarding amenities and agreements, and not once did her name ever come up. In fact, Marnie and Seth seemed to forget that she was there altogether. When it came time to sign the lease, both Marnie and Seth, the latter of whom had spoken very little during the interview, placed their names on the contract. Celina then printed out a single copy and handed it to them, along with their keys. "Thank you, and welcome to our community!"

As they left the building, Lenore heard Marnie tell Seth, "Call Augusten and tell him we're ready."

"Okay." Seth pulled out his cell phone and moved into the grass while Marnie and Lenore walked back to the car.

"I hope you're not offended that we didn't include you on the rental agreement," Marnie apologized in her familiar saccharine voice. "You see, Celina is a devout Catholic, and I didn't want to offend her by having her see that my son and his girlfriend are living together unmarried."

"Ah." Lenore did not know what to say to such an asinine excuse. If Marnie had stated her reasoning to be circumventing residency laws or tenant fees, Lenore would have accepted it, though not necessarily condoned it. That, however, seemed like a move directly taken from the playbook of Lenore's previous boyfriend, whose name she could no longer recall. *How gullible do people think I am?*

"I just didn't want you to be concerned about that." Marnie nervously tapped her fingertips together.

"Not at all." Lenore flashed a phony smile. She saw Seth pocket his cell phone in the distance before he raced over to join them.

"Augusten's on his way," Seth said.

"Who's Augusten?" Lenore asked.

"He's a good friend of mine, and he's agreed to help us move in." Seth rested his hand on Lenore's shoulder. "I bet you're really going to like him."

Seth and Lenore went to the new apartment by themselves, while Marnie stayed behind to wait for Augusten. Once inside, Lenore could see that the apartment was indeed small, even without any furniture in it. The carpet was a dull brown color and the ceiling was spackled with stucco in a texture that reminded her of cottage cheese. Seth took Lenore by the arm and gently pulled her to the back of the apartment.

"Mom says she wants the bigger bedroom for herself, but we don't need much space for what we'll be doing there." He gave her a lewd grin.

"Doesn't that bother you?" Lenore asked.

"Doesn't *what* bother me?"

"The room thing."

"I don't understand."

"You know…" Lenore took a moment to find a tactful way to bring attention to Marnie's uncanny sense of etiquette. "Never mind."

"No, tell me what you mean." He gave Lenore an angry look that she had never seen him give her before. They were interrupted by the front door opening and Marnie calling for Seth and Lenore to help move things inside. Seth groaned and reluctantly headed for the living room. "Can't I take a break for *five freaking minutes?*"

"Where are you going to take a break?" Marnie fired back. "All the furniture is out here!"

Seth dropped his head into the palm of his hand. "Damn it, Mom… why do you have so much shit?"

"I've sacrificed to provide for you for twenty-two years! I think I'm entitled to treat myself to something nice now and then…"

Lenore cringed. *Oh God…I hope they're not always like this.* She found it oddly convenient that they never saw fit to engage in heated arguments over petty nonsense around her until she was stuck with them. *Maybe it was a mistake to do this…* She walked into the living room to do her part, then froze when she saw the stranger standing in the doorway.

He was tall and husky, with pale skin and unkempt, somewhat shaggy brown hair. He smiled when he saw Lenore, causing a strange sensation of familiarity to sweep over her. "Hi, I'm Augusten. You must be Lenore."

Lenore blinked and snapped out of her trance. "Yeah, I'm Lenore. Nice to meet you."

Augusten reached out to offer his hand, and she shook it. "Seth has told me a lot about you."

Lenore chuckled. "Good things, I hope."

"Of course."

They headed out the door to bring in the boxes and furniture, and Seth soon joined them. "We should start with the big stuff," he suggested. "Do we have a dolly?"

While Seth and Augusten moved the heavy pieces of furniture, Lenore examined the latter carefully. *I could have sworn I've seen him before,* she thought, *but where? If he lives out here, there's no possible way I could have known him…I must have just seen someone who looks like him on my old campus or something.*

Once the mattresses, chairs, couch, bookshelves, and dressers were securely set in their new spaces, Lenore helped the men move the smaller boxes and her own meager bin of belongings. She was rather annoyed by how much space Seth and Marnie took up with their own useless knick-knacks, but since they were the ones paying for the apartment, it stood to reason that they would call the shots. *Once I find work out here, I'll be able to contribute more. And once I contribute more to the household, I'll have more say.*

After everything had been transferred from the vehicles outside to the new apartment, Marnie thanked Augusten for his help. "I wish I could give you some sort of financial reimbursement for your trouble," she lamented, "but I'm a little strapped for cash this month, what with the security deposit and the storage unit…"

"Don't worry about it, Marnie," Augusten said casually. "That's what friends are for."

"I can order some fast food for you or something, if you'd like."

Lenore pondered that statement for a second. *Where is she getting the money for fast food if she can't afford to pay him?*

Augusten shook his head. "Thanks, but I better get going. I need to help my mom install a new stopper in her toilet tank."

Marnie smiled sycophantically. "You do so much for so many people, Augusten. You really are a peach."

Augusten grinned bashfully. "I'm just doing my part as a good friend and a child of God." He turned to Seth. "You should take Lenore up to Holder's Game Shack sometime on a date. Just because you're living together doesn't mean that the honeymoon has to end."

After saying their goodbyes to Augusten, Seth came up to Lenore and draped his arm around her shoulders. "We did it!" he exclaimed proudly. "We're finally in our new home together."

Lenore forced a weak smile. *Well, this isn't exactly what I signed on for…but I've come too far to turn back now. Besides, this is only the beginning.*

# CHAPTER FIVE

Three months had passed since Lenore moved into the tiny two-bedroom apartment with Marnie and Seth Horvitz in Citrus. During that time, she had tried her best to find a job with her meager Sociology degree, but she was either overqualified or not quite qualified enough, and eventually she resigned to taking up the bulk of the housekeeping until an opportunity for paid work presented itself. Marnie took full advantage of the transitory arrangement, as she was unaccustomed to doing such chores as routine household maintenance or washing dishes by hand. Seth had seemingly never been asked to do a menial task in his life; it amazed Lenore to see that it did not come as second nature for Seth to pick up after himself, when she, the child of a compulsive hoarder, had learned to adapt to real world expectations long ago. Marnie, of course, provided lengthy but vague Freudian excuses as to why her son was prone to bouts of social ineptitude.

"Seth had a very difficult childhood," Marnie had told her on one such occasion, as Lenore stood captive to her diatribe while washing the dishes. "His dad had some difficulties, and when he died in 2002, we had trouble with money…" Nevertheless, she clearly had some underlying resentment for her spoiled son. "Seth always had trouble with other kids at school, so I would have to be his friend when no one else would. And he repays me by constantly talking back to me and throwing his weight around." She sighed. "At least now he has someone comparable to him to share his interests with."

Lenore wanted to tell Marnie that Seth's unfavorable behavior was a direct result of permissive parenting, but she knew better than to point out the elephant in the room when the roof over her head was at stake. Instead, she attempted to redirect the conversation. "What about Augusten?"

"Augusten is a good guy, and it's a wonder how he can put up with Seth sometimes." Marnie sat down on a chair by the kitchen table. "He's a bit awkward, though, and a little uncouth…but he's a big help when it comes to moving things or fixing appliances. Still, I think Seth is happier having a female companion. Someone he can share his aspirations with."

Of course, Lenore knew what Marnie actually meant. Seth was just happy to have someone he could sleep with all the time—or rather, someone he *assumed* he could sleep with any time he wanted. Though Lenore had loved the passion during the days they spent living in their respective mothers' homes, she became less enamored once they were finally living together due to the stress of her new arrangement and the exposure to Seth's true colors. Like many of Lenore's lovers before him, Seth was initially hostile to the sexual rejection, but eventually he realized that he did not have the physical stamina to fan the flames on a nightly basis anyway, and agreed that they should take a break once in a while to prevent their bedroom activity from going stale.

Outside of sex, Lenore was limited in the variation of recreational activities at her disposal. She was largely housebound, but she had a limited number of books with her, all of which she had read at least twice before. Seth worked full-time as an engineer for a small office and Marnie's job as a court interpreter left her with sporadic hours, so Lenore's social interactions largely consisted of listening to Seth's lengthy, tiresome rants about coworkers he never bothered to compromise with or Marnie's out-of-touch lamentations on life. She had lost phone service within a month of moving to Citrus, as she could no longer afford to pay the bill herself, but there was no one of consequence that she had hoped to keep in contact with anyway. She had tried calling her mom at some point, only to find that the number had been disconnected. Calling the number with the aid of a blocking service yielded the same results, so she figured that her mother finally had to cut her phone service in order to save money. Once again, Lenore was truly alone in the world as a consequence of her own failed ambitions.

As Lenore was lying in bed one afternoon, apprehensive over whether or not Marnie thought she was doing enough around the house, she wondered, *How is it that my life turned out exactly the same as it was before, even after I've strived to change both myself and my situation?* She rolled over. *Maybe God hates me. Maybe this is why religion has never worked for me...or why I've never fit into religion's mold.* She closed her eyes and lost track of time, which caused her to shriek out in surprise when Seth burst into the room.

"Sorry. Did I wake you?"

"No, I was just zoning out." Lenore sat up. "Are you home early, or is it after five already?"

"It's five-thirty." Seth reached into his jeans pocket. "I have a little something for you."

Lenore narrowed her eyes. "I'm not in the mood for this, Seth..."

"Huh? No, look." He pulled out a silver key ring with a large bronze key and a medium silver key. "I made copies of the house and gate keys. Now you can go outside and run errands or whatever."

"I can go out?" Lenore was so enthused about the prospect of relieving her cabin fever that she ignored Seth's implication that the keys were intended to further her responsibilities of servitude.

"Yeah. Just make sure to let Mom know when you're leaving. You can leave a sticky note on our bedroom door or something."

"Okay, that's doable."

Seth leaned over Lenore suggestively. "*You* are doable."

Lenore rolled her eyes, but since Seth had basically done her a favor, she figured they might as well have a little fun. She leaned back on the bed, pulling Seth with her.

Her first mission in venturing outside was to take a walk around the perimeter of the apartment complex, just to become aware of her new surroundings. It had been so long since she had set foot outside that the spring sun instantly blinded her, and it took a few minutes for her eyes to fully adjust. Once her vision was clear, she took in the view of her immediate area. The interior of the apartment complex was a large square, consisting of buildings that were two stories high with salmon pink walls and brown doors. The center of the square was essentially one large patch of grass, symmetrically divided by two perpendicular walkways that met in a diamond. Each section of grass was contained by a loose wooden fence about two feet high, with random cultivars of trees and bushes sprinkled among each of the four sections.

The front gate was made of vertical metal bars painted brown to match the doors and covered with a pink shingled awning. The back gate, which led to the parking structure and waste disposal units, consisted of the same metal bars but was covered with foliage in place of an awning. Two long, tapered evergreen trees guarded the back gate, resting parallel to one another. They seemed out of place in the complex, standing so uniform and stretching so far into the sky that Lenore could swear they reached all the way to heaven. As she walked toward the back gate and passed between the two trees, Lenore felt a strange sense of déjà vu, much like she had felt upon meeting Augusten. She looked up at the sky between the trees, watching them extend unnaturally into the atmosphere in a perspective that did not seem possible. She glanced to the side, and out of her peripheral she noticed a strange blink, like the glitch of a computer graphic, that gave the impression of a crease or crack in the sky. She dismissed it as a bizarre trick of the sunlight, then proceeded out the back gate to begin her adventure.

The parking area was a series of tiny garages that tenants were forced to share. It was a constant source of misery for Marnie, who made sure the rest of the household was aware of her suffering in no uncertain terms. Lenore had no patience for the woman's first world problems, and had she been aware of them before arriving in Citrus, she would have found any excuse not to move in with Seth, or so she told herself on her walk. There was another gate by the dumpsters that led outside of the complex altogether, into an alleyway behind an abandoned elementary school. Lenore followed the alleyway out into the street, then crossed the street and found herself walking the length of a different cul-de-sac. One side of the dead-end street was closed off by a tall wooden fence, where a wild tangle of bougainvillea bushes crawled up the hidden side and reached over to create a canopy over the sidewalk. As Lenore walked under the foliage, she thought, *I know this place…I've seen something like it before.*

It reminded her of the childhood days spent at her maternal grandparents' home in Glendale. She and Armin would ride up and down the sidewalk on their tricycles, and as long as they stayed on one side of the street without turning any corners, they could ride as far as they wanted in either direction. Sometimes Lenore would walk up the sidewalk without her tricycle and discover idiosyncratic landmarks with childlike wonder: a patch of extremely soft grass near the curb, a lone willow tree in someone's yard, or a veil of leaves that potentially led to another dimension, which in reality was the end of the sidewalk and her cue to turn around. Lenore missed those days at her grandparents' house, the one place where she had ever felt truly safe. When her grandfather died, it was the end of her innocence—once he passed away, Lenore knew that she could never go back to the security she felt as a child.

Lenore came to the end of the bougainvillea tunnel and met with a length of barbed wire curled across the top of a chain-link fence. *I guess this is my cue to turn around and go home…but what am I going home to?* She knew that she could run away if she wanted to. She could take a few meager items for survival, or perhaps nothing at all, and walk away from the Horvitzes for good. *But where would I go? I can't go back to my mom and Armin…I couldn't face the humiliation. Besides, I don't even know if they would let me come back. I'm as good as dead to them.* She turned to complete her circle around the cul-de-sac, but as she came around to face her direction of origin, she found everything across the street unrecognizable.

*Maybe I walked further than I realized.* Lenore knew she had to retrace her steps somehow, so she continued her trek in the logical direction. She glanced back at the bougainvillea tunnel, but suddenly, it appeared to be merely a long wooden fence with vines growing over the top. *I must be dreaming. Or maybe just hallucinating.*

Lenore walked down the path before her until she came to a bus stop, where a man wearing a tight black T-shirt tucked into black slacks stood with his back against the sign and a black backpack at his feet. Although she normally made a point to avoid eye contact with lone strangers, the man seemed clean-cut enough to be trusted. "Excuse me," she began. After she caught his attention, she continued, "Can you tell me how to get to the Westchester Apartments?"

"They're right around the corner." The man gestured behind his back with his thumb. "Are you new around here?"

"Yeah," Lenore confessed. "In fact, I just moved to those apartments, but I went out walking and got lost. And I don't have a cell phone anymore, so I can't call my boyfriend to give me directions back home."

"You should be careful out here. It's easy to get lost, or to run into people who will do you wrong."

"So far, everyone I've met out here is nice."

"That's good. But it's easy to misjudge people's intentions sometimes."

"True..." Lenore had already experienced that firsthand.

"I have something to give you." The man crouched down to open his backpack, and after rummaging around he presented Lenore with a holstered can of mace. "I originally intended this for my daughter, since she works graveyard at a gas station, but her boss said she couldn't have it with her on her shift."

Lenore tentatively reached for the mace. "Are you sure? Is it okay for me to have this?"

"You're well within your right to defend yourself," the man explained, standing up and straightening his slacks. "Hopefully, you won't need to use it, but just in case...there you go."

"Thank you." Lenore was confused, but she accepted the mace anyway.

"You're welcome. Just make sure you give it a vigorous shake before you use it, and hold it as far away from your face as possible. And after you spray it...*run.*"

"This is very generous of you."

"I'm just doing my part as a good person, the way God intended. My name's Daniel, by the way."

"I'm Lenore."

"Lenore? That's a pretty name. Take good care of it."

"Thank you." Lenore glanced at the Westchester Apartments in the distance. "I have to go home now. It was nice meeting you."

"You too. Maybe we'll meet again." He closed his eyes and gently rested the back of his head against the bus stop sign. Lenore put the holster of mace in her pocket and started walking back toward the apartment complex.

*Maybe God is watching out for me. After all, they say that angels often take the form of common men, and that they appear in the lowliest of places to the most insignificant of people.* A small shadow fluttered over the sidewalk in front of Lenore. At first she dismissed it as a bird, but then looked up to see a large butterfly—yellow with black stripes and a swallowtail. It was the largest butterfly she had ever seen, and it was fascinating to behold. She felt a strange sensation telling her that there was something special about that butterfly, or rather, that type of butterfly which she should be aware of. *Where have I seen one of these before? Why can't I seem to remember anything anymore?* She was tempted to follow it around, but did not want to risk becoming lost in the residential jungle of Citrus again. Instead, she followed its flight pattern with her eyes, watching it rise high into the sky until it disappeared into the bokeh of light and leaves in the trees above.

When she finally made it back to her complex, the sun was already beginning to set. *Seth should be home from work soon.* She fished around in her pocket for her new keys and unlocked the front gate, then trudged back to the apartment to see what new responsibilities were in store. The front door was already unlocked and left open, presumably by Marnie to let the fresh air and sunlight in through the screen door. Lenore let herself in and headed for her bedroom, where she quickly stashed the mace in one of her drawers, between two layers of clothing. She had no intention of telling Seth about the encounter with Daniel or the mace, much less Marnie.

Seth arrived about an hour after Lenore returned home. Some trivial incident at work had set him off, so he was not in the best of moods, and he was eager to take out his frustration on anyone who dared to cross his path. He strode over to the kitchen and opened the refrigerator.

"Who moved my chocolate milk?" Seth demanded, slamming the refrigerator door hard enough to make the containers inside rattle. Lenore did her best to ignore him, instead opting to lose herself in the twisted fantasy of Franz Kafka's *The Trial,* but Seth insisted on crashing and stomping about as he went through the kitchen, louder and louder, until she had reached her threshold for tolerating his tantrum. She sprang from her seat, book still in hand, and paced over to the kitchen, where he was helping himself to a plate from one of the cabinets above the sink.

"What the hell is wrong with you?" Lenore cried. "You're acting like a child!"

Seth stared at her in shock, like a toddler who had just received an unprovoked slap from an otherwise loving mother. It may very well have been the first time anyone had called him out on his behavior. "Maybe if you didn't yell at me, I wouldn't act this way."

Lenore's eye twitched nervously. "What are you talking about? You do this shit all the time, and I can't stand it."

Seth marched up to Lenore menacingly, forcing her to take a step backwards. "Why are you being such an asshole?"

"You think *I'm* being an asshole?" Lenore parted her lips gave her head a subtle shake in disbelief. *Good lord, not even Armin is this dense.* "How am I being an asshole?"

"If you have to ask, then you already know the answer." Seth shoved past Lenore and opened the food pantry, pulling out a package of sandwich cookies.

"That...makes no sense." Lenore considered hitting him in the back of the head as hard as she could with *The Trial*, but she refrained. Defeated, she slipped back into the living room and sat down with the intention of resuming her book. Seth came out of the kitchen moments later, bringing his plate of cookies and a tall glass of milk, and sat down next to Lenore.

"Don't call me a child," he warned. He set his plate and glass down on the coffee table with such force that a few drops of milk flew out and splattered Lenore's legs. She said nothing as he inhaled his snack and turned on the television.

A few hours later, after the three apartment mates had finished their nightly tradition of a late dinner and two prime-time drama shows that Lenore took little more than a passing interest in, Seth found it within himself to apologize for upsetting his girlfriend.

"I forgive you," Lenore assured him, although she was certain that he did not understand what he was apologizing for.

"But I want you to watch how you talk to me," Seth added. "I won't tolerate being called names." Lenore opened her mouth to protest or defend herself, but he cut her off. "And I don't think Mom would appreciate hearing you talk to me that way."

"What's that supposed to mean?"

"That depends...what do you want it to mean?"

Lenore did not want to disappoint Marnie, although she could stand the woman even less than Seth. Every day was a constant subjection to inconsequential rambling about how Marnie perceived she had been wronged in some way: how she could have been killed by a reckless driver who almost plowed into her at an intersection because she failed to use her turn signal, or how Seth did not think to commit to some task he had never been asked to do, or how the apartment's maintenance crew was not available at her beck and call to help her change a light bulb.

What grated on Lenore's nerves the most, though, was how ignorant Marnie was of other people's struggles. She would make a callous remark about homeless people being too lazy to find a proper job, then wax dramatic about how she ought to qualify for food stamps because her annual income was just over the poverty line, all while she was able to afford cable and order kitschy collectible trinkets over the internet on a regular basis—there was one week in which Lenore answered the door to find a parcel on the doormat every single day, each time addressed to "Marnie Horvitz."

In addition, Marnie would casually belittle Augusten behind his back on the occasions he was called upon to assist her with some blue-collar undertaking that her own spoiled son was incapable of doing. She had no shame in looking down on him for being grungy, or when he spent leisure time with Seth, citing him as being too loud or having tastes in entertainment that were not quite as refined as her own. Of course, Marnie was nothing but pleasant to Lenore directly, but Lenore took these criticisms personally, as both she and Augusten came from humble backgrounds and shared many parallels in their respective social standings. Lenore wondered if Marnie had similar reservations about her and her life prior to moving to Citrus. It seemed that Marnie had the demeanor and limited world view of a southern plantation belle, lacking only the accent.

Life with the Horvitzes was not all bad, though. For instance, Seth would sometimes take Lenore out for a day trip on the weekend if there was a particular activity he wished to engage in, and Marnie would occasionally treat her to something exquisite, like a dessert or a new article of clothing. All Lenore had to do in return was keep the peace and keep the apartment in running order, and satisfy Seth's physical needs often enough to show that she cared for him. If she gave Marnie and Seth their circuses, they would provide her with bread—and to one who is starving, a piece of bread can mean the difference between life and death.

# CHAPTER SIX

Lenore was sitting in the comfortable reclining chair in the living room, reading a book after having finished vacuuming and eating lunch, when she heard a knock at the front door. *It's probably another stupid package from Amazon,* she mused bitterly as she rose to answer the door. *Maybe that woman wouldn't be in such dire straits financially if money didn't burn a hole in her pocket...* When she opened the door, she was greeted instead by two young men in their late teens or early twenties, both dressed in collared white shirts with short sleeves and dark slacks. One of the men had close-cropped blonde hair and a purple necktie, and the other had curly brown hair and a blue necktie. Each wore a black name tag that bore their surnames in stark white font: *Elder James* and *Elder Piper*, respectively.

*Missionaries.* Lenore recognized these particular missionaries by their attire. They were members of a church denomination that her mother had always warned was heretical.

"Why are they bad?" Lenore had asked.

"They practice and believe things that go against the teachings of the Bible," was her mother's non-specific example.

"Does that make them evil?"

"It makes them not true Christians."

Lenore's mother had then given her an array of Protestant literature to further her quest for religious knowledge. Every bit of it was written from a point of view that was biased in favor of whichever sect of Christianity the author hailed from. She had yet to come across any objective information on the denomination in question.

"Hello," greeted Elder James. "Do you have a moment?"

"Sure." Lenore was not overly interested in being preached to, but she did not want to be rude.

"Is it just you here?"

"I'm the only one home right now."

"Oh, okay." Elder James took a pen out of his pants pocket and wrote on a business card. "We would like to invite you to come to church with us this Sunday. Here's the address." Lenore opened the screen door slightly so he could hand her the card. "It starts at nine in the morning."

"Is there a time we can come back later?" Elder Piper asked.

"I don't know," Lenore replied timidly. "I'll have to run it by my husband and see what he thinks." That was her go-to excuse for getting rid of solicitors, whether she was in a relationship or not.

"Okay, that's a good idea," Elder James agreed. "We'll see you later, then."

"It was nice meeting you," Elder Piper added.

"You too." Lenore waved to the missionaries through the screen as they walked away. As soon as they were out of sight, Lenore heard one of the bedroom doors open.

Marnie sauntered into the living room. "Who was that?"

"Just some missionaries." Lenore sat down and returned to her reading.

Marnie groaned. "Can't they bother someone else?"

"They wanted to come back, but I gave them the excuse that I needed to 'talk to my husband' about it." Lenore gesticulated with air quotes to illustrate her citation. "That usually suffices in getting rid of people."

Marnie softened her demeanor. "I've had to use that excuse myself a few times in my day. It's frustrating how people won't leave you alone unless you bring a man into the picture."

Lenore let her guard down a little. "Yeah, it is."

"Don't get me wrong. I think it can be good to be part of a church, to have that sense of community and all...I just wish they wouldn't bother me in the middle of the day to tell me about it."

"Yeah." Lenore did not know what else to say, so she left the matter alone.

When Seth came home, Lenore told him about the encounter with the missionaries. "I'm not a religious person," Seth responded casually. "I don't believe there's a God. But I get why people would want to believe, so I won't judge."

"I am a little curious about their church," Lenore admitted. "But I already scared them off with that old 'let me talk to my husband' line."

Seth's eyebrows twitched, as though Lenore had planted a seed of suggestion in his mind. "You know, maybe it's time we actually considered marriage."

"Huh?" Lenore eyed him with confusion. "What do you mean, 'time'? There's no preordained measure of time that requires a relationship to end in marriage."

"That's not what I meant. I'm just saying that since we love each other and plan on being together forever, it makes logical sense."

Lenore did love Seth, or at least, she loved being in love with him.

She loved their passion, so long as it was not overwhelming, and she loved the more platonic moments spent watching television together or going out on day trips. However, his immaturity and his symbiotic relationship with his mother, combined with Lenore's own uncertainty with her life, made the concept of matrimony completely out of the question. "I suppose that's something we'll have to talk about."

"You mean, like setting a date?"

"That's one small part of it." Lenore could tell that her explanations were soaring straight over Seth's head, and she tried to dodge the conversation. "That would take considerable planning."

"It doesn't have to be a huge wedding. Maybe just a few friends and family, and some cake."

Fortunately, Marnie walked by to interrupt them. "Seth…I need to speak with you."

Sent furrowed his brow like that of a caveman. "*Now* what?"

"Come with me for a moment."

Seth reluctantly followed his mother into her bedroom, and Lenore heard the door close behind them. *They're probably talking about money again,* Lenore assumed. For some reason, Marnie would go out of her way to keep Lenore in the dark about financial matters. Lenore initially assumed she chose to speak to Seth directly because he was the one paying half of the rent, but one time when he relayed the conversation to her, Marnie became quite irate and gave Seth an earful over it. Not only did Lenore feel left out of the loop, but she considered it an injustice to have life-affecting information intentionally kept from her, especially since she was the one Marnie relied on to take the rent check up to the main office every month—which aroused more suspicion in Lenore, considering Marnie's excuse for excluding her from the rental agreement.

Lenore was tempted to listen through the door, which was easy given the weak soundproofing it gave, but she knew enough about Marnie's conniving nature to guess that it had something to do with Marnie not earning enough as a court interpreter to cover something or other and needing to borrow money from Seth. Besides, she knew that Seth would pass on the information in spite of his mother's meddling. She was beginning to think that maybe she had been too hard on Seth, that maybe he was more a victim of circumstance than a willing participant in Marnie's manipulation, and that perhaps there was a way to help him break free.

The same two missionaries returned the following week, after Lenore failed to show up for services. "Do you have a moment to hear a message about Jesus Christ?" Elder Piper asked, and Lenore agreed to hear them out, if for no other reason than to be polite. Since it was against their policy to enter the home of a woman when her husband or another woman was not present, she accommodated them by sitting outside on the old wooden fence as they preached their gospel.

"What is your name?" Elder James asked, and Lenore responded with her first name. "And your last name?"

"Kavaranian." It took some time for her to guide them through the pronunciation, syllable by syllable.

Elder James handed Lenore a pamphlet with a picture of Jesus Christ rising out of his tomb. "Do you know about the restoration of the true church?"

"No," Lenore replied, tentatively accepting the pamphlet. "What's that?"

Elder James cleared his throat and held up his own copy of the pamphlet. "Well, you see, there was a time on this Earth between the martyring of the last apostles of Jesus and the restoration of the church that was known as 'the Great Apostasy.' During this time, there was no one left who was properly qualified to perform the ordinances necessary for salvation, such as baptisms." He turned a page in his pamphlet. "Then, in 1820, there was a farm boy who wanted to know which religion he should follow. There were so many different variations of Christianity, and he wanted to know which one was the right one."

Lenore's eyebrows lifted in pleasant surprise. "I've experienced that myself."

Elder James smiled. "I think it's a common desire to want to know the truth about our Creator." He turned another page in his pamphlet, which showed a painting of a young man kneeling in the forest and two similar-looking apparitions of men in white robes appearing faintly at the top of the grove. "This boy wanted so badly to know which church to join, so he went out into the woods to pray about it—to ask God which church was the true church to join."

Elder Piper took the pamphlet from Elder James and continued the story. "Both God and Jesus Christ appeared to him in a vision, and they told the boy that none of the existing churches were true."

Lenore normally reserved a level of skepticism for Biblical tales, considering most of them to be allegorical or descriptions of unknown phenomena as understood by the people of the time. However, the idea of a miraculous story taking place in a somewhat modern era intrigued her, and she wanted to hear more.

"Some time later, in 1829," Elder Piper continued, "he was called upon to be a prophet of God. This means he had to be given the priesthood—that's the proper authority to perform important spiritual ordinances."

"Like baptisms," Lenore remembered.

"That's right." The missionaries went on to briefly explain a little bit about how the church restored by that truth-seeking farm boy was the same true church that continued to the present day. Lenore had already learned some information about that church's founder from her mother's books, but they were mostly bent on highlighting polygamy and other sordid details that had long since fallen out of fashion with the present-day version. It felt refreshing to learn about the church firsthand from an actual member.

"Tell me, Sister Kavaranian," Elder James said, "do you like to read?"

Lenore's eyes lit up. "I *love* to read!"

Elder James presented Lenore with a blue paperback book with gold lettering and a faux leather texture on the cover. It was not more than a couple hundred pages long, which would be easy for Lenore to peruse if it was interesting enough. "This book is another testament of the Gospel of Jesus Christ. It tells about a people who came to live on the American continent, before the Native Americans, and how they prepared for the coming of Christ."

"We won't spoil it for you, though," Elder Piper joked.

"Go ahead and read it," Elder James continued. "You should feel a sensation prompting you, and you can pray for yourself to know if what you read is true."

The three of them concluded their meeting by folding their arms across their chests and bowing their heads in a prayer led by Elder James, which started by addressing God as "Heavenly Father" and finishing with the phrase "...in the name of Jesus Christ, amen."

After the missionaries left, Lenore immediately opened the book and began reading the preface. It had been so long since she had read a new book of any kind that she would have accepted it even if she had no interest in learning more about their religion. As she read through the first chapter of the first book, she found her mind moving off into tangents she had never before taken into consideration: what if the reason why she never felt right in other Christian denominations was because they really were the wrong churches? What if she really could change her life for the better? What blessings would come to her from becoming a member of that church? There were footnotes at the bottom of each page in her new book, many of which cross-referenced verses in the Bible. Lenore went into her room and pulled off her dusty copy of the King James Bible, which her father had given to her years ago. She sat down in the comfortable chair again and continued her studies until Marnie went into the kitchen to start dinner.

Later that evening, Lenore combed through her belongings until she found an old gray dress that she had not worn since she was eighteen. It was the most church-appropriate dress she had with her; anything remotely similar was locked away in the storage unit that she had no access to. *I knew there was a reason why I kept this thing.* She woke up early on Sunday morning—Seth was still asleep—and threw it on with a pair of black pantyhose and a little eye makeup before following the missionaries' directions to the church.

She passed the local supermarket, Valley View Super Store, and committed its location to memory as she strolled by several other churches along the way. Some of the churches were quite humble and indistinguishable from a modestly priced house, others were ornate with stained glass windows and intricate architecture, and a few were specially tailored to provide sermons in other languages. Finally, Lenore arrived at her destination—a medium-sized brown building with a mosaic façade of various small stones. There was no cross or other distinctive marker denoting it as a Christian church save for the name emblazoned on the side of the building in gold letters. The main entrance to the church was behind the building, which Lenore accessed through the parking lot.

Once inside, Lenore found herself walking down a brightly lit hallway hung with various prints and paintings from the church's lore and culture. Several happy people greeted her on their way to the chapel, which awaited at the end of the hallway. The missionaries were there to greet her and hand out programs for the talks to be given that day.

"We're so glad you could make it, Sister Kavaranian," Elder James cheered as he handed her a program.

"Thank you." Lenore took the program and sat down in a central pew toward the front of the chapel. She closed her eyes, taking in the holiness of the atmosphere, until the bishop spoke to welcome them all to sacrament meeting. It had been a long time since she had set foot in a church of any kind, but she always remembered that those she had attended held long, drawn-out sermons from the pastor based on his interpretation of the Bible, with some hymns thrown in for good measure. Instead, Lenore was surprised to hear talks given by members of the church themselves—men and women from all walks of life—about how the Gospel of Jesus Christ had a real-world effect on their lives. Some of the speakers were even moved to tears by their experiences, and Lenore could tell that they were truly in love with their Heavenly Father. After listening to their testimonies, she knew that she felt the same way. When sacrament meeting ended, the missionaries met up with Lenore to tell her about the rest of the church meeting schedule, which included a short Gospel Topics class and then a sex-segregated meeting where the women of the church would discuss how to be better daughters of God. Although Lenore did not understand everything explained in those classes, they gave her a better insight into the congregation's morals and belief system. She spoke briefly with the missionaries about another time to meet, then walked home in high spirits.

The walk back to the apartment was peaceful. The leaves of the trees glittered in the sun as the wind tossed them about and the few cars passing by on the road were uncharacteristically quiet. Lenore took a shortcut through the street behind the apartment complex, where she had encountered the canopy of bougainvilleas, but the cul-de-sac she had lost her way in was no longer there. *Maybe I'm confusing this with a different street,* she surmised, seeing nothing but a plain-looking set of condominiums lined with knotted tree trunks. She glanced into the windows of each condominium, taking note of the way they were decorated—balconies full of potted and hanging plants, glass panes adorned with decals, and brightly colored curtains. Her wistful admiration of these dwellings was not unlike her experience as a child, living in unfavorable conditions and walking past rows of apartments, wishing she could live in any of them alone and be at peace. *Perhaps I will live in one of the second story residences, looking out onto the street below with a glass of wine in my hand and a smooth jazz record playing on the stereo...and maybe someone to share it with. Could that someone be Seth?*

When Lenore returned, Seth asked her about her experiences at the church, and Lenore answered fondly. He seemed to be accepting of her joy until he asked, "So, do you seriously believe that stuff?"

"You knew I believed in a higher power when we got together," Lenore reminded him. "And I thought you said you didn't care what other people believed."

"Well, yeah, but I thought you were going to be a hypocrite like other Christians."

Lenore was once again baffled by Seth's ignorance, but she remained tactful. "You should come with me sometime. You might enjoy it."

"Thanks, but no thanks. You do what you want, though."

Lenore continued her missionary lessons, thoroughly enjoying every new idea that she learned. The missionaries taught her that God had a plan for her: "We start out as souls in heaven, then come to earth as a test, and after we die, we face judgment and get sorted into one of three different tiers of heaven, depending on obedience and faithfulness."

"What about hell?" Lenore asked.

"Well, there is sort of a hell," Elder Piper tried to explain. "It's not really a part of the three kingdoms of glory…it's outer darkness, but you basically have to *try* to get there."

"What do you mean?"

"It's where you go when you know the truth, but willfully turn against it. Blasphemy against the Holy Spirit, so to speak."

"But you don't have to worry about that," Elder James assured her. "You should just focus on attaining the highest degree of glory."

Other missionary lessons followed in the weeks to come. There was instruction on tithing, which Lenore was exempt from because she earned no income to give, and fasting, which was done once a month for spiritual renewal. There were dietary restrictions on alcohol, tobacco, coffee, tea, and drugs, all of which Lenore could do without. The only lesson that made her uncomfortable was the Law of Chastity, which reserved sexual relations for married spouses and heavily encouraged celibate thinking. Although she kept up the misrepresentation of being legally married to Seth, she knew the truth…and more importantly, *God* knew. If Lenore was to do right in the eyes of her Heavenly Father, she knew she would have to take Seth up on his offer to make it official. She explained that to Seth shortly after the missionaries left.

"So, how soon do you want to do it?" he asked eagerly.

"I don't know…I'm not sure that I want to." Lenore fidgeted with the edge of her T-shirt.

"But you just said it was a requirement for your salvation."

"I mean, I'm not sure I want to do it *with you.*"

Seth glared at her. "What the hell do you mean?"

"I mean, you're great as a boyfriend…but you don't really seem… well…" Lenore fished around for the most harmless way to express her feelings, knowing fully that Seth would take offense no matter what she said. "Well, you don't seem *ready* to be what I expect of a husband."

"What are you talking about? I have a job. I buy you things. I *love* you."

"You have an anger problem—"

"*I don't have a fucking anger problem!*" He bellowed with such force that the walls shook, prompting Marnie to come out and investigate.

"Seth? What's going on out here?" She looked legitimately concerned, and Lenore's blood ran cold.

"Lenore just told me that she doesn't want to marry me. *Ever.*"

Marnie's eyes narrowed. "Oh? And why is that?"

"That's not what I said!" Lenore cried defensively. "I was just saying that he needs to work on certain behaviors before I feel like we're ready to marry."

"Certain behaviors?" Marnie glared at Lenore, making her feel small and helpless. "Like *what?* He's only a year younger than you are!"

"Go on." Seth nudged Lenore sharply in the shoulder. "Tell her what you *really* think of me."

Lenore's lips trembled as she spat out the first thought that came to mind. "It's a personal argument—nothing to worry about."

Marnie was not satisfied with that answer. "Look, *Lenore*," she hissed contemptuously, "maybe you thought this was going to be some sort of free ride away from whatever shithhole you grew up in, but that's not going to fly." Lenore was left speechless, as that was the first time Marnie had ever spoken to her in such a manner, but Marnie continued. "Seth clearly loves you, and you'd be hard-pressed to find another man who can provide for you the way he does. And Seth…" She turned to her son. "You're going to have to make a decision that I myself made when I married your father—you're going to have to accept that you might love someone who doesn't love you as much. Can you live with that?"

Lenore felt as though she would cry, but refused to give either Marnie or Seth the satisfaction. Seth, on the other hand, smiled self-righteously in spite of his mother's backhanded advice.

"Now go," Marnie finished, "both of you get the hell out of my sight!"

The next few days were uncomfortable for all parties involved, so Lenore did her best to stay away from the spiteful matriarch. After that, Marnie seemed to forget that the incident had ever happened, but Lenore was much more weary. The day came at last when she was ready to be baptized, but when speaking about it to the missionaries, they told her that some new information had come up, and that she would have to speak to the bishop.

"What happened?" Lenore demanded.

"We came by to check on you the other day when you were out," Elder James explained, "and your mother-in-law very harshly dismissed us. She also stated that you don't actually live here and you're not actually married to her son."

It was a bolt out of the blue. *That smarmy bitch.* "When can I see the bishop?" was all she could think to ask.

"We'll arrange for you to meet with him after sacrament this Sunday," Elder Piper promised. "You might want to bring your…husband."

Seth agreed to go with Lenore to church, and surprisingly, did not seem bored by the rituals of the congregation. He was friendly to her acquaintances, even going as far as engaging them in polite conversation, and bowed his head for prayers. Lenore was apprehensive throughout the meeting, not out of fear for Seth's actions, but of what was to come in the bishop's office. *Perhaps I should tell the truth…but I can't bear to be shunned by God's true church. I can't let these people down...I can't lose this. It's all I have left.* After sacrament meeting, Lenore and Seth waited silently in the hallway until the bishop called them into his office.

"I understand that the missionaries were told by a family member that you two aren't really married," the bishop addressed calmly. Lenore swallowed harshly, and Seth leaned forward to initiate a response.

"Well, you see," he replied matter-of-factly, "my mom's memory isn't what it used to be, and she sometimes forgets important things that have happened. I think...I think she must have forgotten that we got married."

Lenore thought that was one of the stupidest excuses she had ever heard, but Seth's embarrassment was legitimate enough that the bishop believed him. "So," the bishop continued, "how long have you two been married?"

"About six months," Lenore lied. That was the amount of time she had been living in Citrus.

"And it's been a good six months?"

"We've had a few bumps, but otherwise, yeah." Lenore patted Seth's leg for emphasis.

"Well then, may the Lord continue to bless your good fortune." He smiled and folded his hands together, and Lenore felt a tremendous weight being lifted from her chest. The bishop asked the couple a few more mundane questions about their work and home life, then agreed to schedule a baptism date for Lenore.

Once Seth and Lenore were beyond anyone else's hearing range, Seth whispered, "This is with the agreement that we're going to be married soon. Otherwise, I'll turn back around and tell your bishop that it was all a lie."

*God has given me a second chance,* Lenore realized. *I need to repay him by keeping his commandments.* She nodded slowly and replied, "Okay."

# CHAPTER SEVEN

After an interview with one of the high-ranking clergy addressing the commandments to keep and filling out her contact information for the official records, Lenore was baptized a member of the church. It only took a moment for one of the brethren to fully immerse her in the warm water of the baptismal font, but in that stolen second she felt the presence of God letting her know that whatever had happened in the past, in spite of what others had tried to convince her, she could change. She rose from the water, high on the grace of God, to praise and congratulations from Seth and the congregation. In that instant, she saw everyone as a child of God and became enlightened by that revelation. As she climbed out of the font, she saw Seth watching in awe from the other side of the glass. She smiled at him and silently resolved to use her newfound spirituality to help liberate him from his mother's toxic nurturing.

During sacrament meeting the following Sunday, several members of the priesthood laid their hands upon Lenore's head and confirmed her as a member in front of the congregation. Once again, various people in the church came to express their happiness and offer their friendship, as well as answer any questions she might have as they came up. She was overjoyed at how welcoming everyone was, but she did not expect random members of the church to show up at her door with various foods and well wishes.

"How the hell do they manage to get past the gate?" Seth wondered, although he and Marnie were both delighted by the free gifts. Lenore was certainly grateful, but she was left scratching her head over how these complete strangers knew where she lived. It was only after receiving a stapled stack of papers titled "Ward Directory" with the names, addresses, and phone numbers of all the church members that she realized her contact information was community property.

That posed a problem for Lenore. First of all, there were times when she would stay in her pajamas all day, or Marnie would saunter about in alternating states of indecency, when the new missionaries or Sister So-and-So would show up out of the blue. Second, it made her paranoid about having her secret found out, so she had to stay consistent with the story she gave before her baptism, lest someone report that all was not as it seemed. Given her close call with the bishop, she began to make sacrifices to appease her guilt: she changed her diet to reflect the scriptures' suggestion that she eat meat sparingly and convinced Seth to respect her wish to remain celibate until their inevitable marriage, which he was convinced would be soon. During that time, Lenore began to realize that she and Seth had little compatibility outside of the bedroom. In addition to his Peter Pan complex and anger management issues, she found that each of them had vastly different interests that the other did not respect.

There was another secret that Lenore was hiding from the church, and from everyone else: she was starting to develop soft feelings for Augusten. It started with subtle differences in his and Seth's attitudes, like the time when Lenore tripped and accidentally knocked a bowl of chips onto the floor. Augusten immediately asked "Are you okay?," whereas Seth's first instinct was to berate her for not being more careful. Then there were the moments where he actively asked for her opinion or seemed legitimately interested in an anecdote she recalled, on the rare occasion that she was able to remember something from her past. Sometimes she found herself so lost in her daydreams of him that she would wander around the apartment aimlessly and forget what she was supposed to be doing. Of course, she tried to capture her thoughts the second she became aware of them, but during her church meetings she had learned that it was fine for someone to have taboo feelings as long as they refrained from acting upon them. Still, her emotions troubled her spiritually.

Although Lenore could not pinpoint the exact moment she began falling for Augusten, she was sure that the catalyst was when the Horvitzes invited him out to eat with their extended family during the winter holidays. It had been a favor for Seth, who felt sorry for Augusten because his biological father had passed away a couple of Decembers prior, and Marnie saw it as an opportunity to appear charitable. They drove to his house to pick him up, where they found him sitting on the bed of a white pickup truck, listening to his MP3 player in a meditative state. His hair was damp, presumably from a recent shower, which created gentle waves around the framework of his round face. He wore a short-sleeved cerulean dress shirt and dark gray jeans, and even Lenore had to admit to herself, *He cleans up nicely.* Marnie was about to gently beep the car's horn when he opened his eyes, almost as if he could sense their presence.

"I'm sorry, Augusten," Marnie remarked casually. "I didn't mean to disturb you."

"It's okay," Augusten assured her as he rose to take his designated spot in the passenger's seat. "I was just listening to some smooth jazz. It helps me to relax."

That caught Lenore's attention immediately. *He likes the same music I like!*

"I'm not too familiar with smooth jazz," Marnie replied, which was her roundabout way of saying that it was beneath her.

"Does your car have an MP3 port? I can show you some if you'd like."

"I don't know. I'm not sure what all these buttons are for."

A quick scan of the radio panel revealed that Marnie's RAV4 did indeed have an MP3 player port, and she acquiesced to his request.

"This is an album by Grover Washington, Jr. It's called 'Winelight.'" As Augusten played the music, she was once again flooded with the strange premonition that she was in familiar territory. Seth remained silent, most likely nursing a headache from the voluntary fast he always took in preparation for a sizable feast. The drive out to the restaurant made him sleepy, so he rested his head in Lenore's lap as she stroked his hair absently, enjoying the soft music and the myriad of lights on the skyline outside, varying in brightness and tone.

They met Seth's family at a high-end Chinese restaurant south of Citrus, about an hour away from the apartment. Among the clan were Seth's older cousin Gloria and her husband Pedro, Gloria's friend Raquel and her husband Peter, and Seth's Aunt Jo and Uncle Garrett, the latter of whom was the older brother of Seth's late father. All of them were rather well off, with each of the younger women marrying into money and the elder couple having acquired their finances through Garrett's job as a lawyer and possible subterfuge. As always, everyone was extremely warm in receiving Lenore, but by that point she knew better than to trust them.

Gloria and Pedro had agreed to foot the bill for the entire group, so when it came Lenore's turn to choose a menu item she purposely chose one of the cheaper selections. It did not matter, as everyone was sharing from all of the platters, but she wanted to do her part accordingly. While waiting for the food to be presented, she listened intently to the family's most uninteresting conversation.

"I've taken to shopping in thrift stores lately," Raquel declared in a hoity-toity manner. "Now, don't get the wrong idea—you can really find some amazing antiques there!"

Lenore had been receiving all of her books and clothes, save for undergarments, secondhand for most of her life and found nothing shameful about it, but she said nothing and continued to humor Raquel's ostentatious anecdote.

"I found this amazing, peridot—" she pronounced the word as "peri-*dough*" "—green crushed velvet couch the other day…of course, it was a little out of my price range, so I arranged for the shop owners to place it on layaway…"

Seth remained quiet, as he was clearly just as bored as Lenore, but being family gave him the privilege of not having to feign interest. Augusten, on the other hand, seemed genuinely interested in what Raquel had to say, even going as far as contributing to the topic at hand.

"Sometimes they'll let you negotiate a lower price," Augusten said. "And once you've established some kind of assertiveness with them, you can pretty much get good deals on everything."

"I'll have to remember that." It was unclear whether she was being sincere or dismissive, but Augusten took it as the former.

"I used to do work for a thrift store, moving furniture and stuff. I picked up a few trade secrets along the way."

"I've had a few acquaintances that worked in the clothing industry," Gloria piped up. "These darling little Persian ladies…oh, the things I learned from them!"

Thus, the conversation continued about the quaintness of provincial people and places until dinner was served.

"It must be nice, living in a culture that eats only with chopsticks and soup spoons," Marnie mused. "It takes all of the guesswork out of memorizing the difference between the cake fork and the salad fork."

Lenore had grown up reusing plastic cutlery and would just as soon use Marnie's silver cake fork to scramble her eggs, and had to roll her eyes just a little.

"I wouldn't know a salad fork from a pitchfork," Augusten laughed. "Though to be fair, either one would suffice."

Out of all the smiles and chuckles elicited from his joke, only Lenore's was legitimate. She met his gaze by chance and realized that his eyes were the same color as hers, the only dark brown eyes in a sea of blue and green set by the rest of the participants. Having Augusten as company was the only thing making the dinner party bearable.

At some point, the conversation shifted from lower-class guilty pleasures to existentialism and spirituality. "Lenore is part of an interesting church," Seth offered, and all the attention moved to her.

"What kind of church?" Pedro asked.

Lenore was reluctant to speak, but nonetheless happy to share her religious beliefs with others. "I don't think it's unlike other Christian denominations," she began, "except that we believe in an open canon to our doctrine. And we have some different views on the afterlife."

"Like what?" Gloria asked.

"Well, we believe that we existed as spirits in heaven before we came down to Earth, and that our time here on Earth is a trial of knowledge and obedience that determines where we go when we die."

"So, just heaven and hell stuff?" Jo inquired. "That sounds pretty normal, I think."

"Well, it's more Universalist in that regard. We believe that there are three degrees of glory in heaven—the highest is for those who've had all of their ordinances done and lived by God's commandments. The second is for good people who didn't necessarily believe in God or follow his church, and the lowest is for everyone else."

"Kind of reminds me of Dante's *Divine Comedy*," Raquel observed. "Is there room to move up in those levels?"

"Sort of. We can do vicarious ordinances on behalf of those who died without them, up until Christ returns."

"Interesting," Augusten interjected. "I have kind of a similar theory about God."

"You can't have a 'theory' about God," Seth interrupted. "A theory is a scientific method."

"Well, science and religion aren't necessarily mutually exclusive," Augusten continued. "Maybe what we know as 'science' is actually God's plan put in motion. If he's supposed to be omniscient, it would make sense that he would have some sort of a system for things to work out over a long period of time."

"I don't think God is Rube Goldberg," Seth argued.

"I thought you were an atheist," Lenore remarked.

"I am," Seth replied, "but it's just...I don't know. What's your *hypothesis,* Augusten?"

"Well, you see," Augusten went on, "as Lenore was saying, life on Earth is like a trial until Jesus comes back. But my take is, what if the Apocalypse already happened, and we're just living like normal, trying to find our way back to God?"

"But what about other religions?" Pedro asked. "Is there one that's right, and that's the key to the Kingdom?"

"That's the thing," Augusten continued. "Maybe all religions are a path to hell, so to speak. Think about it. Christianity came about as a reformed sect of Judaism, then got huge and corrupt. The Protestant Reformation came out of that, and now that denomination is in power. They say that God works in mysterious ways, but maybe it's more like subtle ways. Maybe we need to find our own way to God...or recognize the signs when he finds us." He lowered his head in humility. "But that's just one idea."

After dinner, Augusten personally thanked all of his hosts for the generosity of having him, and Garrett, who had mostly stayed silent during the mealtime, seemed taken aback that someone associated with Seth and Marnie was capable of expressing gratitude. The extended family offered awkward hugs and handshakes all around, then Augusten, Lenore, and the Horvitzes piled into the RAV4 to go home.

As they embarked on the hour-long drive back to Citrus, Lenore took note of the skyline again. She watched the lights blink out on the buildings nearest the freeway, presumably shutting down for the evening, and then the silhouettes of the buildings themselves began to disappear. *It must be an optical illusion...or maybe I'm finally going insane after living with these assholes for so long. How long has it been, anyway? A year now? I don't even know what year it is anymore.*

Augusten thanked Marnie for the ride and dinner invitation as he was dropped off at his house, and once Marnie had safely rounded the corner out of his street, she began to complain about him. "I know Augusten likes to be involved in the conversation, but boy, sometimes he's really blowing smoke. I mean, all that talk about how we might be in purgatory and how all churches are corrupt and evil...he sure likes to think he knows everything, doesn't he?"

"That's what all religions are to me," Seth replied evasively. Lenore instinctively kept her mouth shut, letting her anger sizzle inside her chest.

Marnie sighed, almost as if she felt guilty for voicing her criticism. "But Augusten really is a nice guy with a good heart...I bet if he lost some weight, he would be a real lady killer."

*Augusten is perfect the way he is,* Lenore thought, and as he crossed her mind once more, she felt her heart racing.

The next few meetings at church featured at least one sermon apropos to her dilemma: "The Family is Part of God's Plan," "Strengthening the Bond Between Husband and Wife," and the most ominous, "Eternal Marriage in the Temple."

"When a man and woman are married during their lifetime," her Gospel Topics teacher, Brother Stevens, explained, "that marriage ends when one or both of them die. But when a couple is sealed in the temple, that marriage will last for time and eternity."

"What if my husband dies before he can become a member of the church?" Lenore asked.

"Well, like with baptisms and other ordinances, sealings can be done vicariously through the living."

"So I'll still be sealed to my husband forever?"

"Yes. As long as you were married in this lifetime, you can still be sealed."

Lenore's heart sank. The idea of being married to Seth for the rest of her life filled her with existential dread, but being stuck with him for eternity made her wonder when the "happiness" part of God's "plan of happiness" was going to kick in. "Do you have to be sealed, or even married to receive Christ's salvation?"

Brother Stevens picked up his Gospel Topics manual. "That's a good question, Sister Kavaranian..." He opened the book to the table of contents, then leafed through until he came to the chapter on the subject. "Well, previous prophets have spoken on the subject, speaking about the blessings on the sacred covenant of marriage. It is something that all people should strive for, and it is ordained of God: 'And in order to obtain the highest, a man must enter into this order of the priesthood'— that is, the new and everlasting covenant of marriage—'And if he does not, he cannot obtain it.'"

"I see. Thank you, Brother Stevens." Lenore smiled in gratitude, but inside she was crestfallen.

"And thank *you*, Sister Kavaranian, for your insightful questions."

It felt great to leave church that Sunday. Lenore took her time on the way back, enjoying the beauty of nature, but her mind once again wandered to thoughts of Augusten. *If God really wants his children to marry and have families for our happiness, then why does the idea of marriage not make me happy? Or is it that the idea of marriage to* Seth *makes me unhappy?* She strolled down the sidewalk, noticing that the tough, spiky sod that she was accustomed to had been replace by the soft, silky grass she remembered from a house near her grandparents' home. She went through the alleyway again, and as she passed through the two trees at the back gate, she couldn't help but wonder if Augusten was thinking of her, too, or if he felt that same sense of déjà vu whenever they were in proximity of each other.

"I'm back!" Lenore called as she entered the front door. The living room was empty and quiet, which was not unusual for a Sunday afternoon. *Seth is probably still asleep,* she figured, and let herself in through their closed bedroom door. To her surprise, Seth was awake and fully dressed for the day.

"I talked to my mom this morning," he said gravely.

"Oh?" Lenore could not disguise her concern. "What happened? Is everything okay?"

"She wanted to know why we haven't gotten married yet, even though we've been talking about it for months."

"*You* and *I* have been talking about it, but what business is it of hers?"

"She's been paying for your accommodations, and she has no money left in her savings to move out into her own place."

"How is that *my* problem? I've been trying to find a job since I got here. And if she's so worried about me being a financial burden, why does she go out of her way to keep that information from me?"

"When we get married, we'll be entitled to certain benefits that can help us out."

Lenore's jaw wavered in disbelief. "Your mother is pushing us to get married so we can go on government assistance, and she can keep bleeding her bank account on bullshit she finds on the internet!"

"This has nothing to do with my mom!" Seth screamed with such strain that his face turned red. "You promised that we would get married after I saved your ass in the bishop's office last spring. I even agreed to let you take your—your vow of chastity, or whatever. And now, I see the way you look at Augusten—"

"You think I'm lusting after Augusten?" Even if it was slightly true, Lenore would never admit it.

"It doesn't matter, because you're *mine.*" Seth took a step up to Lenore, causing her to instinctively step back and hit the wall. "You need to set a date for us to get married, and it needs to be soon. Just a trip to the courthouse with me and my mom—you can even wear white."

"Fine." Lenore sidled away from his entrapment. "Tell me when you want to do it, and I'll do it. But remember, this is *my* wedding, too. At least give me the dignity of picking out a new dress for the occasion."

"Fine. Mom will be more than happy to accommodate you if you ask her."

"No, I want *you* to do it. If you're gonna be my or anybody's husband, you better cut that umbilical cord."

A knock at the front door interrupted their argument. Lenore rushed to answer it. There were two new missionaries at the door—one was a short blond who looked as though he was still a teenager, and one who appeared to be of Latino descent. Their name tags read "Elder Matthew" and "Elder DeLuna," respectively.

"Hello," greeted Elder Matthew. "Do you have a moment to share a message about Jesus Christ?"

Lenore scratched her head. "I'm already a member of your church, though."

"Oh." Elder Matthew regrouped, then tried again. "Is there anything we can help you with spiritually?"

"Not right now, thanks. I have to go." She bid the missionaries a rushed goodbye and closed the door.

# CHAPTER EIGHT

The rainy season had come around again. Lenore had always loved the rain, as did most people she was acquainted with, but she loved the rain even more after associating it with Augusten. She closed her eyes and allowed her mind to wander back to a time shortly after she realized her feelings for him, when they had been socializing indoors on a Saturday afternoon. She, him, and Seth had been watching internet videos in the living room when it spontaneously started to rain, prompting the trio to drop everything and run outside to enjoy it.

"We probably look like idiots out here, standing in the rain with no jackets or shoes on," Augusten laughed.

"I don't care." Lenore was too grateful for the end of a dry spell.

They came across a tree with an outstretched branch, and Augusten challenged each of them to try and touch it. Of course, he could reach it without effort, being much taller than the others, but Seth had to jump up to touch it. Lenore could not reach it even by jumping.

"Seth, give her a boost," Augusten suggested. Seth attempted to launch her into the air by having her step on his interlocked hands and thrusting them upward, but she only succeeded in stumbling.

Augusten came up behind Lenore. "Is it okay if I pick you up?"

"S-sure," Lenore consented, and he gently lifted her by the waist until she grasped the tree branch. She momentarily swung around on the branch with her legs flailing, then dropped to the ground. She had not given much thought to the fact that Augusten had put his hands on her until after he went home, but once she realized it, she was euphoric.

While Lenore tried her hardest not to think of Augusten in an inappropriate way, she could not control her dreams about him. These dreams were not always sexual, per se, but oftentimes a sign of a failed connection: sometimes the objective of her dreams was just to reach out and touch him, other times she wanted to call out to him but was rendered mute. The dreams always left her wanting more, feeling a frustration she had not felt in years—more than a mere sexual frustration, but rather a longing for a complete companionship. *It seems like I can have a man who satisfies me physically or a man who satisfies me emotionally, but never both.*

Lenore felt trapped in her world. She was trapped in her relationship with Seth, coerced into setting a date for cold courthouse nuptials in the fall. That gave her the opportunity to prolong the inevitable under the guise of having adequate time to plan. She was also trapped in her church, becoming more disillusioned by the day as the focus settled on families, marriage, following the leaders of the church, and the importance of sacred ordinances rather than salvation or the love of a deity. Lenore began to feel the spirit less and less, which must have sent a subconscious signal to the higher-ranked members because she was once again bombarded with church visitors and missionaries looking to go over lessons with her. She began to wonder if she was somehow trapped in her own mind, with a glitch in the system that placed latent memories on endless repeat.

Seth had wasted no time telling Marnie the "good news" about his wedding date, and Marnie followed Lenore around as she completed her chores, waxing poetic about the upcoming marriage ceremony as if to rub salt in her wounds. "Once you two are married, you two will be able to apply for food stamps," Marnie cooed, blissfully out of touch with the severity of the decision to wed.

"That's something." Lenore had no desire to feign excitement, but she was not naïve enough to voice her actual opinion, either.

"You can invite your family," Marnie prattled on. "And I'll take you to pick out a dress and flowers. Just don't get anything purple, because that's bad luck."

"But purple is my favorite color," Lenore protested.

"How about a nice shade of blue? Blue has always represented eternity…" Marnie droned on about wedding dress superstitions and Lenore continued to humor her, focusing instead on the rhythm of the rain and the tasks before her, until it occurred that Lenore could use Marnie's credulous nature against her.

"I'll keep those options in mind, but I really think I should pray about it first. If I want God to bless this union, I need to have a sign from him that I'm on the right track."

Marnie smiled. "What a novel idea!"

Truthfully, Lenore had been praying hard all along. She had prayed for God to take her unwanted feelings for Augusten away, and she prayed for him to make her love Seth again. She poured through her scriptures, both biblical and of the new gospel she had received; the latter told nothing on the concept of love and the former was contradictory at best. The missionaries would continually press for her to ask questions, but she began to develop the impression that her questions were arousing suspicion among the leaders of the congregation, so she plastered on a Stepford smile and told them repeatedly that nothing was wrong, that everything was fine, but the stress was slowly cracking away at her resolve.

The following Saturday, Marnie took Seth and Lenore to a nearby clothing outlet to try on dresses.

"Here's a lovely one." Marnie held up a knee-length blue dress with sleeves that stopped at the elbows.

"Hmm, maybe." Lenore thought that the dress looked like a sausage casing, and not worth the thirty dollar price tag.

"How about this one?" Seth held up a white halter top.

"That's not a dress," Lenore pointed out.

Seth lowered the top back into the shopping rack. "I still want to see you wear it…"

In all honesty, she did not care what dress she wore because she would be miserable just the same. They continued searching for a suitable dress during the next couple of hours, but went home empty-handed.

"Don't worry," Marnie assured her, "we'll come back another time. The wedding is still a long way out."

It seemed that the only peaceful times in Lenore's life were those when both of the Horvitzes were out of the apartment, and even then it was rare. On one such occasion, as Lenore was coming out of the shower —her one place of solace—she heard someone banging on the screen door. "Leave me alone!" she cried, "I'm already a member of your church!"

"It's me, Augusten!" called the voice from behind the door.

*That's right. He was supposed to come help Marnie move some stupid piece of furniture she bought at the import shop.* Lenore jumped and hurriedly ran to answer it, almost tripping over the couch in the process.

"Sorry," she apologized, "I thought you were the missionaries again. Marnie and Seth aren't back yet, but you can wait for them inside." She opened the screen door to let him in, admiring his rain-dampened hair.

"If you want to get rid of them for good, answer the door naked. I've never done it, but I hear that works."

"I'm not sure about that."

"True. In your case, you'd probably get them to come by more often."

Lenore blushed. "That would be counterproductive, wouldn't it?"

Augusten sat down on the couch. "Congratulations, by the way."

"On what?"

"Your engagement to Seth."

"Oh…" Lenore was disappointed that Seth had told Augusten about the scheduled wedding date. "Thanks, I guess."

"I take it you guys have worked out your problems?"

Lenore sat down next to Augusten. "What all did Seth tell you?"

"Nothing. I just observed that you weren't entirely happy with him."

Lenore sighed. "I don't know. It's just that every time I try to make my life better, it ends up exactly the same."

"Like how?"

"Well…" Lenore took a moment to figure out the best way to phrase her idea. "Remember when we went to the Chinese restaurant, and you were talking about how maybe we're all in some sort of purgatory?"

"Something like that. It's just an idea."

"Well, I kind of feel like that with my life. And I can't remember exactly what my old life was like, but I just have this…this *feeling* that I can't escape." Lenore pondered again on her next thought. "You know, everything changed that one night when there was a blood moon."

"Blood moon?" Augusten's eyes widened.

Lenore was sure that he thought she was insane. "Yeah, I just remember there being this bright red moon a few years back or so, and after that, things started to get weird."

"Weird? How?"

Lenore did not want to tell him about the strange optical illusions that plagued her outings, lest he assume that she was suffering from schizophrenic episodes. "I can't really explain."

Augusten thought long and hard for a minute. "The blood moon…that was back in December of 2012, right?"

"Yeah, I think so."

"And that was one of those days that supposedly the Mayans predicted the world would end, wasn't it?"

"Might have been."

There was another knock at the door, which Lenore once again rose to answer. That time it was the missionaries, but Elder DeLuna was the short teenager, though retaining his dark complexion, and Elder Matthew was taller with light-skinned Hispanic features. "Hello," greeted Elder DeLuna, "do you have a moment to share a message about Jesus Christ?"

"Who's there?" Augusten called from the couch.

The missionaries looked past Lenore concernedly to see Augusten looking over his shoulder. Not wanting to risk confrontation, Elder Matthew sighed, "We'll come back later this week."

After dismissing the missionaries and closing the door, Lenore sat back down on the couch. "Maybe my own guilt is eating away at me."

Just then, Seth and Marnie came through the front door, carrying groceries and take-out from the local Mexican restaurant. "Oh, Augusten, you're already here," Marnie observed.

"I just got here two minutes ago," Augusten lied. "Where's the bookcase you wanted me to move?"

"It's in the car," Marnie replied. "Lenore, would you mind putting the groceries away? Here, Augusten, I'll show you to it."

Once Marnie and Augusten were gone, Seth grabbed Lenore by the arm. "What did you two talk about while I was gone?"

"Nothing. He said 'hi' to me and I told him you guys weren't back yet."

"That's still too much conversation."

"Well, what was I supposed to say to him?"

"*Nothing!*"

Lenore ripped her arm away from Seth's grasp and went to the kitchen to put the groceries away, concentrating intently on her task to keep her mind off of her indignation. Once the majority of the work was done, Seth slowly entered the kitchen. "Lenore?"

"Yeah?" Lenore answered flatly.

"I'm sorry," he mumbled dejectedly. "I don't want to fight with you all the time."

"Then why *do* you?"

"I don't know…it's just frustrating for me, still living with my mom and working a boring desk job that she pushed me into…" He moved closer to Lenore as she stashed the last of the groceries into the refrigerator. "I want you to marry me because you love me, not because you're scared of being homeless."

Lenore stood face-to-face with him. "Why don't you stand up to her?"

"Look, I'm going to tell you something I've never told anyone before." Seth swallowed dryly and took a breath. "My dad didn't really die when I was younger. He went to prison."

"My dad's been in and out of lockdown since I was eleven." Lenore's expression remained unchanging.

Seth proceeded to explain the backstory behind his father's incarceration. It was an abominable secret that caused Lenore to recoil in disgust. "Well, because of what he did, I had to go live with my Aunt Jo and Uncle Garrett for a while, and my mom's dad threatened to cut her out of his will if she didn't divorce my dad. My dad was the one person my mom loved more than anyone on the planet, and she gave him up for me. Now I feel like I have to pay her back for her sacrifice."

Lenore stood in silence, mouth agape, bewildered at how anyone could be so overwhelmingly blind to the truth. Any respect that she still had for Marnie was gone, and she began to sympathize with Seth. She gently pulled him into an embrace, and he held her tightly.

"I'll marry you," she whispered, winding her fingers into his curly hair. "And I'll get you away from her." *Maybe this is the way it has to be,* she lamented internally. *Maybe this is just one of those selfless sacrifices I have to make to get closer to God, like the scriptures say. Besides, this way, I'll always have the chance to see Augusten—it's enough just to see him for a few minutes out of a week.*

There was peace in the household for a short time after that. The rains continued, creating flooded patches in the uneven roads. Lenore did her best to avoid Marnie while Seth was at work, reading or praying in her room until the old woman had left for a job. Nevertheless, Marnie always managed to come home at the most inopportune and least expected times. For the most part, Marnie had ceased her gushing over the impending nuptials, but one day in particular, something she saw on her outing must have triggered her excitement anew. After relaying her experiences and frustrations of the day, she segued into a discussion about life with Seth's father, whose very mention disgusted Lenore in light of having more information about him. Then, the topic turned back to the intrusion upon Seth and Lenore's relationship.

"You know, Seth really loves you," she told Lenore. "You're very lucky to have someone who loves you as much as he does."

"I know." Lenore forced a smile similar to the one she put on for church and fiddled with her fingers.

"And I can see that he's very fortunate to have you, too. It's nice to see that one of his relationship attempts finally paid off."

Lenore quit fidgeting and sobered up. "Other relationship attempts?" She knew that there had presumably been other women in Seth's life, but he had never once spoken of them or even hinted at their existence.

"Well, every teenager goes through their experimental phase, but for some reason, Seth was just determined to find someone to settle down with. It seemed like every time things were about to get serious, those girls just got cold feet and bailed on him."

"How many others?" Lenore could not help wondering who else Seth and Marnie had lured into her current arrangement under the pretense of retaining their autonomy.

"Oh, not many," Marnie assured her. "Seth never was very popular with girls…he had a few intense relationships, but when it came time to move in together, they were too busy with their careers or college. It just seems to be fate that you didn't know what you wanted to do with your life, and you were able to give him a chance."

Lenore stood rigidly, feeling the adrenaline course through her veins in preparation for a fight or flight. "I was *told* I would be able to find a job out here."

"Well, it would be difficult for you to have both a job and take care of your responsibilities here, wouldn't it?"

"So, that was the idea all along? I could have been *anybody?*" Lenore's entire body was shaking.

"I wouldn't worry about any of his past girlfriends. He cut his losses with them as soon as they walked out the door." Marnie rested her hand on Lenore's shoulder, and it took every ounce of Lenore's resolve to keep from slapping it away. "They're off somewhere else, lighting their own personal hells."

Marnie either did not understand or did not care why Lenore was upset. She slowly retracted her hand.

When Seth came home a half hour later, Lenore immediately demanded to know the truth. "Tell me, Seth…why do you want to marry me so badly?"

"I told you, Lenore. It's because I love you and I want to start a family together. It's a symbol of our commitment to each other. Your church teaches that it's next to godliness."

"Why don't you trust me enough to believe that I would be committed to you otherwise?"

"Why don't you trust me enough to get married? I thought you got over your jitters."

Lenore would not budge. "Why is your mom so adamant about us getting married?"

"Leave my mom out of this." His voice began to crack as he raised it.

"She's the one *involved* in this! Is she the reason all of your exes jumped ship?"

Seth narrowed his eyes. "What exes?"

"Your mom—"

*"Don't bring my mom into this!"*

"She told me about the others!" Lenore shouted. "I know she's pushing you to find some poor girl to use as a live-in housekeeper and a means of cashing in on welfare fraud! And if you had any real love for me, you wouldn't have brought me here to be miserable!"

"You think *you're* miserable? I have to deal with you *and* my mom! I've been lonely my whole damn life, and I think I deserve to have someone."

The two of them stood in a silent standoff, glaring at each other hatefully until Seth lunged at Lenore and forced his mouth against hers, gripping her shoulders tightly. As she opened her mouth in shock, he let his tongue in for an instant before pulling away and moving down to her neck.

"I love you, Lenore," he whispered in between kisses. Lenore broke out of her surprised trance and pushed him away.

"You can't solve all your problems with sex. I had to learn that the hard way. Now excuse me." Lenore grabbed her keys and paced over to the front door to slip on her shoes. "I need some fresh air."

Seth did nothing as she ran out the door and over to the front gate. As the rain came down like bullets upon her head, she felt nothing but the desire to leave, to go home to her mother and Armin, to go *anywhere*— but everything looked the same in the gray atmosphere. The streets mirrored one another as she ran down them, with only a few blurry cars to break the symmetry.

*Where the hell am I?* Lenore thought, wracked with panic. She ran past the Valley View Super Store, turning into the street of many churches. Every single church had its doors wide open, and the roofs reflected a dull haze that emulated smoke, though given the downpour it would have been impossible for them to be on fire. The buildings seemed to cry out specifically to Lenore, beckoning her to pick from among them. *None of these religions can help me. They won't save me; they will offer me security for a price. They're no better than Seth or his mother.* At the end of the row of churches was Lenore's own church, the so-called "true church" that had once given her such joy. It, too, received the trial of fire.

*Oh God, I'm losing my mind!* Lenore turned around and ran back to the apartment complex, racing through the flooded alleyway, fumbling with the gate key in the lock, and stumbling through the back gate. She passed between the two evergreen trees and stopped to take a breath. A wave of clarity overtook her as she looked upward, watching the tapered trees reach up to infinity: *I'm in hell.*

Everything changed the night of the blood moon. Lenore remembered waking up in a public latrine to an empty world. She remembered her friends and family turning on her, then Seth exploiting her weakness to traffic her into his mother's household. At last, she was trapped; locked into a cycle of servitude and bureaucracy with the man she truly cared about just out of her reach. To make matters worse, the world around her was falling apart as she felt the presence of God move further and further away, and she knew that if she did not find him soon, it would disintegrate completely and swallow her permanently.

Lenore looked up and saw that the cracks in the sky had become creases, like the folds of a box. She was inside a diorama, and everything inside it was an illusion just for her. She fell to her knees, screaming in agony at the open sky as the rain came down mercilessly.

# CHAPTER NINE

After Lenore's nervous breakdown in the rain, she did not interact with Seth or Marnie again that day until the former came into the bedroom to find her lying unresponsive in their bed. He thought nothing of her suffering, though he usually seemed rather oblivious to her mental torment as a whole. She did not bother to explain her predicament to her boyfriend—if she could even call him that anymore—as she did not expect him to understand, let alone believe her.

As time went on, she started to become disillusioned with the repetitive feel-good messages the church poured onto its congregation for a full three hours every week. Another Sunday at church had her questioning why she was even still attending the services at all, especially since she was beginning to doubt the authenticity of the spiritual dogma. *Is being married really a prerequisite for eternal salvation?* Lenore wondered as the congregation took a moment of silence to pass around the bread and water for the sacrament. *The church seems to think so. But Jesus himself never married, and neither did Paul the Apostle, who is often credited with the founding of modern Christianity. Even still, we are told that almost everyone will go to heaven, and that even the sinners will be blessed in the highest degree of glory if they repent…but if God's unconditional love and the Atonement of Jesus Christ are for everyone, why would we need to be separated into castes the way we are on Earth? And to get to the highest degree of glory, there are all of these rituals, these ordinances, these rules to follow—isn't it enough that Jesus died for our sins?*

Lenore took a piece of bread as the tray was passed down her pew. She always opted for the pieces with the crust, when available, as she imagined that the toughness of the outer edge was symbolic of Christ's suffering, and thus she took it upon herself as a form of mental flagellation. *I look at all these people around me, and I can't help thinking that at least half of them would not be married if it wasn't required by the church. And what of those attracted to the same sex? Or those who prefer to live celibate lives? Or those who aren't pretty or competent enough to attract a mate? Would God truly abandon them even if they are otherwise good people?* The tray of water, poured into little single-ounce plastic cups, was next. Lenore took one and drank it all in one shot, then disposed of the cup in the slot provided. *I don't think so.*

There was yet another talk about God's "plan of happiness," but Lenore found it difficult to focus on. The speaker, an attractive woman who appeared to be in her thirties, droned on about the importance of the covenant of marriage without ever detailing why it was important. "One of our prophets made it a point to tell us not to be overly conscientious about choosing a mate," she preached hollowly, as if reading aloud a well-rehearsed book report. "He said, 'Soul mates are fiction and an illusion; it is certain that almost any good man and any good woman can have happiness and a successful marriage.' So we ought to stop focusing on the idea that we need to hold out for Mister or Missus Right, or that we need to 'try before we buy,' and instead focus on what we have in front of us. How can we make our marriages better? How can we…"

Lenore tuned out the message. The heartfelt messages and stories of the congregation that had initially inspired her and brought her joy were woefully corrupted by the constant parroting of the words of high-ranking church leaders, rather than the glorious message of salvation that the missionaries used to lure her in. In fact, Lenore felt further from God than she had ever felt in her life. *How is it that God wants me to do this for my happiness, when what makes me happy are the brief moments I share with Augusten? Everything with Seth has been either a question of lust or whether or not we meet each other's standards. But with Augusten, it's like I'm sitting outside of all that.* She closed her eyes and smiled at the thought of the tall, thickset brunet with his dark eyes and optimistic demeanor. She imagined the way they sometimes matched each other's gaze and then quickly looked away, how his short brown hair curled about his face when it was wet, and other small details of their interactions that warmed her blood and touched her soul. *With Augusten…I feel free.*

After sacrament meeting that Sunday, Lenore decided to skip the other two sessions and go home early. The other members of the church more or less ignored her as she slipped past them and out through the double doors. Even the missionaries were preoccupied with other engagements, greeting people and giving insight to other converts. She walked down the street of churches and saw that several of the buildings were under construction, though whether they were being refurbished or demolished was unclear. Once she was safely back at the apartment complex, she went to her room. Seth was gone—most likely at the store with Marnie—so Lenore took advantage of his absence and used the opportunity to pray.

She knelt before the bed, hands clasped, head lowered, and began her silent message to God. *Dear Heavenly Father, I come to you with a broken heart and contrite spirit, and I ask of you that you may find it… that you may help me…* Lenore struggled for the right words. *Oh Lord, I ask you to guide me in my time of need, to please help me rid myself of my unwanted feelings for Augusten, if it is your will that I marry Seth, and if it is your will, I ask that you guide me…I ask that you guide me…*

As Lenore became more adamant about her prayer, she found herself falling asleep and falling incoherent with her worship. *Oh Lord, I ask you to guide me in my time of need…to please help me…if it is your will…*

She found herself in a trance, repeatedly asking God to help her with a request that never came, then found her body standing in an unknown bar, wearing a pair of black short-shorts and a fitted black T-shirt with an indeterminate yellow symbol on the front. A black pageboy cap and neon yellow high-top sneakers completed the outfit, and as she adjusted her cap, she saw the bar give way to a row of computers and a lounge set up with an electronic entertainment system in the background.

*This is Holder's Game Shack,* she realized, remembering Augusten's mention of it back when they had first become acquainted. She slowly made her way toward the lounge, brushing past the hordes of vestal geeks who made the venue their sacred kingdom as they crowded around her. Lenore sensed that she could have any of them on a whim, as they teased her with their idiosyncratic brand of appeal, but she knew that something better waited for her just around the corner. Dreamlike and dazed, she trudged forward in the general direction of the lounge area, passing through a strange yet familiar crowd of patrons.

As she approached the lounge, she saw a lone figure in a purple sweatshirt standing next to a dancing game, waiting for someone. She could immediately tell that it was Augusten, and he turned around to greet her with a smile. Without saying a word, he stepped to the side and invited her to play the game with him. He placed the tokens into the arcade as she assumed her position on the button mat. They shot each other knowing glances as they stood side-by-side on their respective platforms, and then the music started. They kept to the rhythm of the beat in perfectly synchronized steps. Lenore's bright yellow shoes glowed on the platform with a surreal light, which gradually began to spread upward.

About halfway through the song, they jumped to switch mats, still keeping time with the music, and as the light flooded the dance floor, they eventually abandoned the mats altogether and began dancing with each other. Lenore leaned close to Augusten, gently shaking her hips, then turned around to grind her posterior against him. Augusten did not try to take the dancing further, but he was not put off by it; he eased into the flow of the groove naturally and allowed her to speak volumes with her body language. The pulse of the beat and Lenore's sensual movement combined to create an aura of sexual tension thick enough to cut with a butter knife, slowly enveloping the dark-clad figures in a white cloud of light.

Suddenly, a burst of darkness dissolved the light cloud, and they were back in Holder's Game Shack. Seth appeared out of nowhere, backed by a crowd from Lenore's church. Lenore and Augusten abruptly stopped dancing and stood uncomfortably close to one another, bracing themselves for an unknown but anticipated threat. Seth opened his mouth to scream something, but no sound came out. He rushed forward with the intention of attacking the couple, targeting Augusten first. Lenore jumped between the two men, and as she tried to fight Seth off, he threw her across the room with unrealistic strength. She crashed into something—a pool table or computer terminal, perhaps—and the flash of white light closed her off from the events to come as she jerked awake and slowly phased back into reality.

Lenore was not quite sure what the dream was supposed to be telling her, but she finally realized a connection that her mind had been trying to make for so long: *Augusten is that man in the purple sweatshirt I met on the night of the blood moon.* All of her old memories flooded back to her —The Edge of Heaven nightclub, the night she spent on the cold floor in the restroom of the park, the disintegration of all her personal relationships, meeting Seth and Marnie—all those months and years of internal hell she had been through. Still disoriented, she wandered into the living room to find Seth sitting on the edge of the couch, watching television and unscrupulously eating processed baked goods straight from the box, one after another. He did not notice her enter the room, and she did not bother him as she went to the kitchen for a glass of water. After rehydrating, she returned to the living room to risk disturbing the human time bomb. "Seth?"

"Yeah?" Surprisingly, he paused his show and turned around to pay her attention.

"Do you remember where you were on the night of the blood moon?" She sat down next to him on the couch.

"What 'blood moon'?"

74

"A few years back, in December 2012…there was some kind of eclipse or something on the night the Mayans said the world was supposed to end."

Seth stuffed another snack cake into his mouth. "How am I supposed to remember something that happened all those years ago?"

"Well…do you remember anything major happening in the months before we got together? A death, a breakup, a power outage…anything?"

"Hmm…let me think." He took a moment to chew and swallow the food in his mouth. "I was probably jerking off in my room, or doing something with Augusten…something completely separate from the first idea, that is."

"You weren't out with some girl?" she prompted. "Or…maybe *looking* for a girl to take home?"

Seth put the box down on the coffee table. "Why are you so interested in this? What were *you* doing that night?"

"That's just it—I didn't remember until just now. I was at a nightclub, and I think you were there."

"I'm not a very social person. Clubbing isn't really my vibe."

"So, I take that as a 'no' then…"

"Maybe you saw somebody who looked like me."

"I don't know." Lenore was not about to admit that she had become acquainted with Augusten before she and Seth entered their relationship, so she tried to steer the conversation in a different direction. "But what about *after* that night? Did things start going to shit for you some time around the new year?"

"Well, life only got hard for me after I met *you.*" Seth narrowed his eyes at Lenore. "So in a manner of speaking, yes, things did start going to shit for me after the new year started."

Lenore let his snide remark go unchecked. "Thank you. That's all I needed to know." Once she knew that he had experienced something to the effect of a downward spiral, she knew that she was not alone in her experience. *We are all in this purgatory or whatever together, trapped in our own personal hells as we are forced to deal with other people trapped in their personal hells. Maybe some of us will escape.* She stood up and left Seth to his devices. *And maybe some of us won't want to.*

She did not know how much time she had left to break out of her strange and nightmarish realm. She did not even know how much time had passed since she had entered it. For all she or anyone else knew, a thousand years had already come and gone; perhaps Christ had completed his reign on Earth and was preparing to take those who believed in him back to heaven, or maybe Christianity was not the one true religion she had been groomed to believe it was. *Maybe there is no "true church,"* Lenore thought, *but if faith in a higher power is any measure of loyalty, maybe I'm not a lost soul after all.*

Lenore changed out of her church clothes and into some comfortable garments she had been fond of in her living years: her favorite slim black jeans, which were still in good condition after all that time, and a white T-shirt featuring a pink crew collar, turquoise stripes on the sleeves, and a screen print of a large strawberry in both colors on the front. She completed the ensemble with her black pageboy cap, pocketed her wallet and keys, and ventured out into the living room to retrieve her shoes. *If I'm going to shuffle off this mortal coil, I'm going to do it in style.*

Seth caught a glimpse of her preparing to leave the apartment. "Where are you going?" he asked, more out of curiosity than suspicion.

"I need to find God," Lenore answered matter-of-factly.

"So, you're having some kind of faith crisis? But I thought you loved that church. You went to such great lengths to be a part of it."

"You're an atheist. I wouldn't expect you to understand."

Seth furrowed his brow. "That's not necessarily true. But you have been going out a lot lately, and that's something."

"What's your point?"

"It's just…interesting, I guess." He paused momentarily in thought, and Lenore was sure he was conspiring against her. "Well, good luck with whatever it is you're hoping to achieve out there. Just be back in time for dinner."

"Thanks. I will." She stepped out the front door and walked out the back gate, noticing the myriad of alternating trees peering over the top of the apartment complex like titans looking down on the damned. The only unchanging trees were the two evergreens guarding the back gate, emitting an emanation of knowledge that rested just out of reach, and Lenore was certain that these trees were somehow the key to unlocking the exit to purgatory.

Lenore took her time on her trek, convinced that what little she could still feel of the Holy Spirit would guide her if she concentrated on it ardently. She walked slowly through the alleyway, past the barren schoolyard, and around the corner where the churches once stood. Many of them were gone completely. Some of the spaces were paved with dirt like a burial mound, while others appeared to have never hosted a building at all. Lenore's church was still there, untouched and standing as strong as ever. She saw two missionaries mounting their bicycles outside of the church, though they were too far away for her to tell whether or not she recognized them. A gentle breeze blew against her, dislodging many leaves from the trees above. The delicate green particles danced as they fell and disappeared before they hit the ground.

Not about to be intimidated again by the optical illusions, Lenore bravely ambled past the church and the missionaries, who either did not see her or were too busy preparing to proselytize that they had no time to acknowledge her. She kept going beyond the boundaries of the church into new and unfamiliar territory, finding small foreign food markets and gas stations with signs that read backwards as if being viewed in a mirror. She did not know why the illusions took on such a bizarre pattern, though she imagined that it was because her mind was deteriorating as her soul was being destroyed. Thus, she was determined to waste no time in finding her way to God. *I have to find a way to get away from all this. I have to find a way to reach him...or at the very least, to contact him without interruption.*

A vast community college came into view, not unlike the one where Lenore had received her Sociology degree long ago. There was a football game taking place, but no sound came from the crowd, and she wondered if they were merely specters of people who once were happy. Still, she pressed on to her unknown destination, her legs numb from the endless walking and her mind drained from the bombardment of strange phenomena she had encountered. Finally, she came to a long street with a single road that turned into a cul-de-sac, and just beyond the end of the long street was a small park. It was devoid of other people save for the handful of cars driving by, and the only other life forms were a sparse placement of trees and a handful of crows, cawing to welcome the sunset. Lenore sat beneath one of the trees and watched the cars, gently entrancing herself in preparation for the great prayer she had come to implore.

"My dear Heavenly Father," she started, then changed her mind. "Dear God, I come to you now in my hour of need. I see before me a multitude of churches that claim to be in your name, and insist on being the only church in your name, but I have no idea which of these denominations, if any of them, are true." She watched the cars on the street before her slowly disappear, one after another, until she was completely alone. Not wanting to be distracted by purgatory's impending collapse, she closed her eyes and concentrated on her mantra. "I have been told that if ever I lack the knowledge I need, I can ask you in faith and I shall receive my answer. If the message I've been given by my church is true on any level, then you have given this knowledge before to one who asked of it...so I ask now, with a broken heart and contrite spirit...which path should I follow to reach you? How will I know which path is the correct path?" She paused briefly, silently listening for the presence of God as some sort of confirmation, then concluded her prayer. "I ask these things humbly in the name of Jesus Christ. Amen."

Lenore kept her eyes closed and maintained her prayer posture long after she had finished delivering her message to God. She almost entered a meditative state when suddenly, she felt a hand rest upon her shoulder. Her eyes flew open in terror, and she immediately whipped around to see who was behind her.

# CHAPTER TEN

"Augusten!" Lenore cried. He stood behind her wearing the same purple sweatshirt he had worn in The Edge of Heaven nightclub the fateful night they first met, large khaki-colored cargo pants that were rolled up at the cuffs, and worn-out gray fingerless gloves. His expression was serious, but not urgent. He gently removed his hand from her shoulder.

"I thought I'd find you here. I knew you would find out the truth sooner or later."

"The truth? You mean, about where we are?"

He nodded. "We're in purgatory." He offered his hand to help pull her up from the ground, and she took it.

Lenore brushed the debris from the ground off of her bottom. "So, you've noticed the weird stuff, too, then. The disappearing buildings, the streets changing…all that crazy shit."

"I think it's different for everyone, but yeah, I've noticed some similar things happening." He looked up at the sky. "For me, it's been little coincidences, like finding new street names that are now the names of people, or brand names of snack products that are now businesses… things stored in my latent memory that are just being drawn upon over and over to procedurally generate this world. Have you noticed that the sky has edges, like a box?"

"Yeah! It's like we're trapped in a diorama or something." Lenore gave a quick paranoid glance to her left and right. "You don't think us talking about it is going to make our punishment worse, do you?"

"I doubt it." He put his hands in the pockets of his sweatshirt. "I've been telling people my theory for a while now, and I haven't had any demons come after me or anything."

"How long has it been going on for you? And what are you doing to try getting out of here?"

"Well, it all started that night of the blood moon." He paused in contemplation. "This could be a long story. Do you want to find somewhere more comfortable to sit and chat?"

"Doesn't matter to me. I don't have anywhere important to be."

Augusten sat down underneath the large tree, and Lenore sat beside him. "Well, like I was saying, it all started that night. I was with Seth, which you probably already gathered."

"I asked him about it," Lenore confirmed. "He denied being at The Edge of Heaven, but I knew better."

"Yeah, he probably would say something like that." Augusten shrugged. "He went out to pick up chicks, because for whatever reason he was bent on finding someone to impress his mother with, which most normal people wouldn't go to a bar for, but that's none of my business. So anyway, while he was out there schmoozing, I was sitting in the back where nobody's gonna bother me, and then I saw you. At first I just wanted to make sure everything was okay with your friend, but then I started to feel some kind of connection to you."

"You felt it too?" Lenore's eyes lit up.

"Yeah, it was strange…I can't really explain it. I wrote it off when I got home, but then when I saw you again back when you were moving in with Seth and Marnie, I knew it wasn't just synchronicity."

"You recognized me right then and there?"

"Sort of. I knew you were familiar, but I couldn't place where I had met you before. Then when you started talking about the blood moon a while back, I thought of the moon I had seen while leaving The Edge of Heaven and it all made sense."

Lenore felt her body physically gravitating closer to Augusten, though she had not moved since sitting down. "I wanted so badly to remember you…to remember what happened. I barely remember anything that went on while I was alive—assuming we're actually dead and not just experiencing hell on Earth or whatever."

"I'm actually not sure if we're alive or not," Augusten admitted. "I considered suicide a few times, but I don't know if that would instantly destroy any chance we have at redemption, or whatnot." He looked down at his hands and began fidgeting with the knit material of his gloves. "So anyway, after that night, I remember waking up the next morning in my bed and everything seemed normal. I went about my day, but something felt off…I remember that a few weeks later, my dad, whom I was living with at the time, suddenly had an aneurysm and died in the hospital a few days later. I ended up having to go live with my mom and her alcoholic husband, and then I met Seth a short time later, one night when I was out blowing off some steam."

"Wait a minute…you met Seth around the same time I did?"

"I don't know, had you not known him very long?"

"I met him in the spring semester at my community college. He and I were in a class together."

"That's odd. I remember he had a girlfriend out here for a time, and we met shortly before they broke up…then he was determined as all-get-out to find a replacement for her."

"That's Marnie's doing!" Lenore interjected, her hands balling into fists. "She's hellbent on pushing Seth to get married so that he can go on welfare and she can use the money herself, while keeping the girl around as a housekeeper. Or at least, that's what I've surmised."

Augusten looked surprised. "I've always thought Marnie was a decent person. It seems to me like Seth is the one who has always been pressuring her, taking her for granted."

"Well, there's a lot going on behind the scenes." Lenore did not want to poison him against the Horvitzes if he considered them to be good people. "But go on, tell me more."

"I don't remember when I first started seeing the optical illusions, but I knew my mom would just take me in to have my head examined, so I didn't say anything. Then I came up with this idea that maybe the Apocalypse did happen, and we just didn't realize it. And now…" He shrugged again. "I guess it was true."

"It's really the only logical explanation for things." Lenore and Augusten watched as the trees and houses in the distance faded into the pink and orange sunset, which seemed to have frozen in place for the entire length of time that Lenore had been in the park. "Gosh, it's too bad we didn't have more time to get to know each other."

Augusten turned to face Lenore. "Well, we're here together right now…what do you want to know about me?"

"Well…" Lenore thought for a moment, then looked up excitedly with her answer. "What's your last name?"

"It's 'Keys.' Spelled like there's more than one key." He smiled shyly, causing Lenore's face to heat up.

"Ah." Lenore looked down at her own hands. "I don't know. I just realized that I've known you all this time and I never did learn your last name."

"It's okay."

They sat together under the tree, taking in the aura of the unwavering pink sky as the world around them slowly shifted. Lenore sat dangerously close to Augusten, feeling his heat emerging from his body in the chill of the perpetual twilight. She desperately wanted to move closer to him, but she did not want to risk being too forward. *I don't understand exactly what's holding me back. I've wanted this moment for the longest time, even fantasized about it against my better judgment. And now, I feel like if I put my arm around him, or place my hand on top of his, or anything like that, I'm going to ruin what we have. And I don't even know if he feels that way about me...* She glanced up at his face, but he continued to stare stoically out into the sunset. *But maybe now's not the time, anyway. If anything happens between me and Augusten, I want it to be the real thing. I don't want either of us to inadvertently take advantage of the other person's vulnerability.* Ultimately, she decided that for once she would live in the present, as it was, and just enjoy what was happening at that point in time.

At last, Augusten broke the silence. "Tell me more about your life."

"My life?" Lenore forced a laugh. "My life isn't that interesting. My life has been one long, bad dream that I now know I'll never wake up from."

"Oh, I know the feeling. But it does get better..." He reached out tentatively, as if to touch the side of her face, but instead shifted into a more comfortable sitting position, accidentally elbowing her ribs in the process. "Sorry."

"It's okay." Lenore turned her head down and away in bashfulness, not wanting Augusten to see her beaming brightly. *Damn, I wish I wasn't so shy around him.*

Trying to shrug off the sudden awkwardness, Augusten brought the conversation back on track. "Well, I was born out here in Citrus, and I've lived here all my life..."

The two of them discussed their respective past experiences, likes, dislikes, and other relevant conversation topics for a length of time. Lenore learned that Augusten had grown up under similar circumstances of poverty and a broken home, had trouble making friends growing up, and someday wanted to become a published author. He eagerly listened to all of her anecdotes, as she could finally recall everything from her old life, and she realized that he was the first person to ever take an active interest in the things she had to say. Naturally, she left out the details of her relationships with past lovers, but she did not hesitate to tell him that she had learned a great deal from those encounters, and he seemed to approve of her stance. She could not recall the last time she had smiled so much, let alone laughed out loud. At some point, she found herself resting against his arm, waking up her feminine instincts by breathing in his scent, but he did not seem to mind, or even notice. *This feels so natural...this feels so right.* She could have lost herself in the moment with him, let purgatory swallow her and spent the rest of eternity melting away with him...but then the discussion came back around to the original subject of their predicament.

"So, if our goal is to find God, then how do we go about it?" Lenore asked.

"I think God finds us all in different ways," Augusten replied confidently. "Maybe that's why I never really went out of my way to find a way out of this place." He sighed. "But if there *is* a way out, and we have to seek it ourselves, I think I'm more than ready to find it."

Lenore's eyes widened. "Now that you mention it, there is a place that I think might hold the key to our escape."

"How?"

"I don't know, exactly…there's this spot in my apartment complex where the trees go on forever, and every time I pass between them, I get a sense of déjà vu. I feel like there's something I can do there, or that it can give me something I need."

"It's entirely possible. I've met a few people out here to that effect."

"People?" Lenore was confused. *Does he have another kindred spirit besides me?*

"Yeah. There was this one guy in particular, he said his name was Paul…I got into a fight with my mom's husband one night and stormed off, and this guy came up to me, dressed up all nicely in black, and asked me if I was homeless. I told him I wasn't, but he said he wanted to help me out, so he gave me a five dollar bill and told me to be careful of whom I trust out here. Shortly after that, I met Seth."

Lenore's blood ran cold. "Something similar happened to me shortly before I joined the church."

Augusten raised his eyebrows. "Maybe they were guardian angels or something, and they were trying to guide us to the right path."

"It's possible…" Lenore's voice trailed off. "Do you think we failed?"

"If we did, we would have been eaten alive in this place by now." Augusten rose to his feet. "Show me this place with the trees. Maybe together we can crack the code."

Lenore stood up beside him. "If I can find the way back now…"

Augusten gingerly brushed her arm. "You'll find your way back. We found each other again without even having exchanged names, so if we're destined to leave this place, we'll do it."

They walked quickly, which eventually turned into running, with Augusten following Lenore's lead. All around them, buildings were falling to decay or rising out of the ground onto floating islands. The sidewalk abruptly ended and Augusten tumbled forward, almost hitting the ground. Lenore stopped to make sure that he was all right. He motioned for her to keep going forward as he paused to catch his breath, but she stayed with him until he was ready to go again. Every car on the street had disappeared and there were no other human beings around, but the occasional flock of crows would soar overhead in formation as a premonition of the chaos yet to come. As they picked up the pace, Lenore reached out for Augusten's hand, which he gladly accepted. The warm touch of his fingertips against her olive hand gave her a much-needed boost of adrenaline, and interestingly enough, Augusten was able to keep up with her. Together they raced into the alleyway and through the first gate.

"The trees I told you about are right over here." Lenore pointed to the two evergreens, which could be seen poking out from the top of the back gate like a couple of green flames. She let go of Augusten's hand to unlock the gate, then he held the door open for her as she stepped into the apartment complex. She stopped between the two trees as Augusten followed her, letting the gate shut behind him, and froze in place.

Seth stood menacingly in the center of the sidewalk, about five feet away from the back gate. He aggressively stared them down and was poised to attack at any given moment. "I had a feeling you were going to see him," he addressed Lenore angrily.

"What are you talking about?" Lenore demanded. "I didn't go to see him, we just met up on the way back."

"Like hell." Seth slowly approached them. Lenore nervously stepped back, but Augusten jumped in front of her protectively.

"If you feel threatened by me, that's *your* fault," Augusten declared. "You've been possessive of Lenore since you first became attracted to her, and now you're threatening to scare her off just like you did with your last girlfriend. Maybe if you treated her like an equal instead of an extension of yourself, she wouldn't feel intimidated."

"Shut up, Augusten," Seth warned. "I'm not going to have you... *preach* to me like I'm a child."

"But you're *acting* like a child," Augusten continued. "If you want to marry this woman, I suggest you man up. Stop projecting your own insecurity and jealousy. Maybe try being her *friend* before you even think about being her husband."

"I didn't ask for your opinion, and I sure as shit don't want it."

"Get lost, Seth," Lenore spoke up, coming forward to stand next to Augusten. "Unless you're going to join us."

"I don't want to do whatever the hell it is you two are doing," Seth argued. "I want you to come spend time with *me,* Lenore. Like a *couple.* Like we're *supposed* to."

"That's all I ever hear," Lenore fired back, "from you, and my family, and religion—always stuff about how I have to change because I'm 'supposed to,' with no clear reason as to *why* I'm 'supposed to.' Is it because society will collapse if I don't conform to it? Is it because God will curse me? Is it because your Mommy Dearest won't have enough money to keep living within her comfort level? How does any of this actually benefit *me?*"

"Because I *love* you, damn it!"

"And what does 'love' mean to you, Seth?"

Seth ignored her question and turned back to Augusten. "You were supposed to be my friend, you fat son of a bitch! My *best* friend, at that! And now you turned my own wife against me!"

"I'm not your wife yet, you self-righteous cocksucker!" Lenore shouted, causing Seth to drop his guard. "Maybe you should listen to Augusten, because he's not wrong."

Seth scowled at Lenore. "You're a whore, you know that?" He growled like a wild animal and rushed up to Augusten, who took a step backwards out of surprise.

"Whoa! Take it easy!" Augusten dodged Seth's attack and pushed him away, but Seth continued his assault. "I'm not gonna fight you, bro. Knock it off."

"Leave him alone!" Lenore wedged her petite body between Augusten and Seth, trying to shove Seth away, but he knocked her to the ground. While she was down, she caught a glimpse of something glistening in Seth's hand. "Shit," she swore as she rose from the ground, "he's got a knife!" She jumped forward and forced her way in front of Augusten just as Seth plunged the knife forward.

Lenore felt the breath taken straight out of her lungs as a cold, white shock overcame her body. First she felt numb, then she felt a gradual pain radiating from her left side. She looked down and saw a red-orange stain rapidly climbing the white fabric of her T-shirt. As she overcame her shock, she saw that Seth's wrist extended past her waist, and only too late did she realize that the knife had merely grazed her and instead sank firmly into Augusten's abdomen. With an eloquent twist, Seth ripped the blade out of Augusten, causing him to stumble backwards and clench his hands over the wound. Blood seeped through his fingers nonetheless, spilling onto the sidewalk and creating a dark discoloration on his purple sweatshirt.

"*Augusten!*" Lenore screamed, feeling her fear and anger boil over.

Breathing heavily to the point of dry heaving, Seth readjusted his grip on the blood-covered knife and leaped toward Augusten once more, blade brandished, ready to finish what he started. Lenore sprinted forward to stop Seth, in spite of her own wound, and succeeded in getting in his way. Augusten regained his balance and bolted for the gate, struggling to wrap his slippery hands around the doorknob. Seth smiled deviously, knowing he had Augusten trapped, and prepared to strike again.

"Seth, there you are!" cried an angry female voice behind him. Seth stupidly turned around to see who was bothering him.

"Damn it, Mom," he seethed, "what do you want *now?*"

"The light bulb in my desk lamp is out," she complained. "You said that you were going to change it first thing in the morning. Now it's dark in my room, and *I* need to do my work."

"Can't it wait?" Seth barked.

"What are you doing that's so important that you can't do one *measly* little thing that I ask you? I worked twenty years in a job that stopped giving me annual raises…" She droned on and Seth continued to argue with her.

In the split second it took for Seth to become distracted, Augusten wasted no time in his effort to open the gate. Once he succeeded, he disappeared into the parking area, leaving a prominent trail of red-orange blood behind him. Lenore ran into the apartment complex to find a telephone with which to call the police. *I can't believe that stupid cow cares more about her superficial misfortunes than the fact that she caught her son red-handed in an attempted murder. But then again, I guess nothing should surprise me about this place anymore.*

Lenore crashed through the apartment and raced to the landline telephone. She dropped the phone as she grabbed it, nearly knocking the service line out of its port. She dialed 9-1-1 as precisely as she could, waited about thirty seconds for the dispatcher to pick up, then explained the situation. After giving her location and hanging up, she ran back out to the scene of the crime.

Both Marnie and Seth were gone by then. Lenore ran back toward the gate, where all of the bloodstains had strangely disappeared. There was no longer any blood covering the doorknob to the gate, which Lenore discovered as she opened it, and there were no bloody footprints leading out in any direction. "Augusten?" she called loudly, wondering if he was hiding out in a vacant garage or even one of the waste disposal units. "They're gone now, and I've called 9-1-1." She frantically searched for any sign of him, but there was not another person anywhere in sight. "Augusten?" she called again, simultaneously afraid to find him lying lifeless somewhere and concerned that she did not know what had happened to him. Overwhelmed, she burst into tears. *"Augusten!"*

# CHAPTER ELEVEN

Lenore raced back toward the apartment, her face streaked with tears and eyeliner, her shirt torn and stained with a mixture of her and Augusten's blood. As she came back through the gate, she noticed Marnie standing just outside of the apartment complex at the front gate, talking to a pair of police officers. She slowed her pace to a power walk to keep her distance while still making an attempt to overhear the conversation.

"Well, I don't know what exactly was going on between them," she heard Marnie say in her usual sycophantic voice. "They must have had some sort of disagreement."

"Thank you, ma'am," one of the officers replied. "We'll see if we can find either of them."

"Okay, thank you." Marnie returned through the front gate as the police officers left. Lenore ran to stop them, to tell them everything that she had seen and heard, but a slope appeared in the center of the complex square, slowing her down. Before Lenore could catch up to them, they had already entered their car and driven off.

The sky was changing from bright pink to a dull shade of violet, reminding Lenore of Augusten's trademark sweatshirt. *Augusten's out there,* she thought, *and for all I know, he's already dead.* She could feel the bile rise up in her esophagus at the very thought of the horrid possibility. *No...I have to find him. I have to find him before Seth does.* Without hesitation, she hurried into the apartment to grab her sweatshirt and prepare to spend the entire night searching for him if she had to.

Lenore burst into her room, half expecting to find Seth waiting for her there, but he was still missing in action. She rummaged through her closet in search of her sweatshirt, and when she failed to find it, tore into her dresser drawers and happened upon the holstered can of mace that the stranger named Daniel—potentially one of the Lord's messengers sent to guide purgatorial souls back to the path of righteousness, as Augusten suggested—had given her ages ago. Lenore knew that if ever there was a time where she might need to use the mace, it would be on the desperate search for her wounded friend. She hooked the holster onto a thin black belt, and when she finally found her missing sweatshirt in the pile of clean laundry she had forgotten to fold, she hurried out of the room to begin her quest. However, Marnie was sitting in the living room, creating a psychological barrier.

"Hello, *Lenore.*" Marnie rarely called Lenore by name, but when she did, she spat it out with such vitriol that it may as well have been a profanity in the old woman's personal lexicon. With that, Lenore knew she was in trouble.

"Hello." Lenore did not know how else to respond.

Marnie took note of Lenore's sweatshirt and shoes. "Where do you think you're going?"

"I'm looking for Seth." That was half-true, as Lenore intended to protect Augusten from his unbridled wrath. "I need to talk to him."

"The police came here, asking about an altercation he apparently had with Augusten that ended in violence. You wouldn't happen to know anything about that, *would you?*"

"That's why I need to find Seth. I…I'm worried about what will happen to him."

Strangely, that answer seemed to satisfy Marnie, as her demeanor softened. "I know that Augusten must have done something to provoke Seth," she lamented. "People don't seem to understand what kind of a person Seth is…what kind of life he suffered through. I think they would understand him much better if they knew the whole story."

"Whole story?" Lenore had a feeling she knew what Marnie was referring to and did not wish to hear it again. She braced herself for Marnie's apologetic excuses.

Marnie sighed. "You see, there was a bit of a controversy surrounding Seth and his father, back when Seth was a child. Now, Seth's father had his faults, you see, but he was a talented man, and most people just couldn't see the good in him…well, my father *hated* him, and after the incident happened, he cut me out of his will!" Marnie's eyes widened with perceived indignation. "I couldn't believe it—I *needed* that money to live on, you know—so I had no choice but to divorce my husband after he went to prison…it was hard on Seth, but I did my best to provide him with everything, and I fear he may have become a bit spoiled in the process. But he's had such a hard life, you really must understand."

"I see." Lenore, who normally trembled with anxiety when left alone to speak with Marnie, felt a sudden boost of confidence, as though she had nothing left to lose. "That's exactly the reason why Seth is so fucked up."

Marnie's mouth opened and closed like that of a fish before she managed to successfully speak. "Excuse me? I did what I *had* to in order to survive."

"And what exactly is 'surviving' to you?" Lenore fired back. "Having enough money to live within your high-end comfort zone? You could have taken welfare for a time if you were really destitute, or maybe found a second job, since your freelance court interpreter bullshit doesn't pay the bills…God forbid you might walk a day in my shoes, or maybe Augusten's, since you think he's so *beneath* you."

Marnie became increasingly incensed. "How *dare* you! I took you in at the *insistence* of Seth, who did nothing but love you more than you loved him! And what have you done in return? Just a few lousy dishes, and not even that well, and you expect a free meal and a place to sleep? That's not going to cut the mustard!"

Lenore pointed an accusing finger at Marnie. "You dropped the ball, lady. Instead of pandering to your son to try and hide the fact that you willingly let his father do something terrible to him, you should have taken that ill-gotten inheritance money and paid for some counseling for that spoiled little sociopath. My dad was a shitty human being, too, albeit nothing like your husband. But nobody pulled a rose-tinted shade over *my* head—I had to learn to deal with life the hard way. That's why I know how to deal with life, while Seth throws a tantrum like a toddler with a neurodivergent disorder every time he's faced with a minor inconvenience. Maybe if you had been a better parent to him instead of acting like he ought to magically know all the common nuances of adulthood that you were supposed to teach him in his youth, he wouldn't have grown up thinking he could get away with murder!"

Lenore watched Marnie recoil into the corner of the couch like an intimidated cat, but she spared no sympathy for the woman who had willingly used her and others for personal gain. "You're a greedy, pretentious, selfish, aging whore who thinks you're entitled to everyone else's money while letting your own slip through your fingers like water. You care more about material items than actual people, and you think you're better than people like me and Augusten, whom you feign admiration for until we do something you don't like, and even then you talk about us behind our backs like we're the scourge of society. You whine about how the world has wronged you while failing to recognize the irony in how you have had no problem putting yourself before others, not the least of which was your own son." As she spoke the words she had longed to use to put Marnie in her place, Lenore felt her body freeze rigidly, her feet planted to the ground like the roots of a tree. She was chained down by her anger, determined to let Marnie know exactly what she thought of her.

A quick glance down at the worn leather couch revealed Marnie in tears, looking older than she had ever appeared in her life. Lenore almost felt bad for the woman, but then she remembered, *This bitch let Seth hurt Augusten.* "What did you tell the cops, Marnie? I know you lied to them to take the heat off of Seth. If Augusten dies…" She trailed off, taking note of Marnie's crumpled form. *This woman was once like me,* she realized in horror. *This is what I will become if I succumb to my misery. She will never leave purgatory, because she doesn't have what it takes to humble herself—not before God, not before anyone.*

"I pity you." Lenore finally broke free of her imaginary shackles, and once again she could move freely. She wanted to say more, but there was nothing more to say that had not already been stated. As she walked toward the front door, she could have sworn that out of her peripheral vision, she saw Marnie disintegrate into a pile of dust.

It was dark outside when Lenore finally made it out of the front door. The stars were entirely concentrated in the center of the sky above the apartment complex. The general oddity of the world seemed to have ceased for the time being; everything was still and silent with the exception of the slightest breeze blowing over at random intervals. Lenore's first thought was to search through the parking area toward the back gate, where she had last seen Augusten, but something persuaded her to exit through the front of the complex instead. When she stepped out into the open, she saw the spotlight of a police helicopter hovering overhead. *They must be looking for Seth and Augusten, too.*

She started down the sidewalk, not quite sure where she was going, and kept alert for any sign of life from anyone. There were a few cars parallel parked on the street, but no one else was outside. A squirrel scampered across the road and into a nearby tree, startling Lenore, but she regained her composure and made it to the end of the street before the sound of an ambulance caught her attention.

*Augusten.* Lenore was certain that someone had found him, although in what condition he was found remained to be seen. The sound of the siren grew increasingly louder, prompting Lenore to throw her hands over her ears as the ambulance drove by. To her surprise, the large white vehicle turned into the cul-de-sac and stopped in front of the apartment complex. Lenore stowed away behind a nearby tree and watched the paramedics roll out a gurney, enter a key code to unlock the gate, and disappear.

A draft settled over the area, forcing Lenore to pull the hood of her sweatshirt up over her head, covering her hat. She pulled the narrow brim down over her face, both as a shield from the wind and a disguise against anyone who might find her whereabouts suspicious, and anxiously waited for the paramedics to come out again. The wound in her side was aching, so she pressed against it with her elbow to dull the pain. Not knowing what else to do, she closed her eyes and began a silent prayer: *Oh God, I ask of you...please keep Augusten safe, wherever he is. Protect him in my absence, no matter what happens to me, and if it is your will, please see that Seth is properly brought to justice. I ask these things in the name of Jesus Christ, amen.* When she opened her eyes again, she saw the paramedics wheeling out the gurney with someone strapped onto it. From her distance, she could not make out who or what was lying on the gurney, but she suddenly felt at ease as the paramedics placed the mysterious figure into the back of the ambulance and drove off. *Thank you, Lord,* she quickly prayed again, and once the ambulance had rounded the corner, she crept back into the apartment complex.

The apartment door was unlocked and the screen unlatched. Lenore was unsure whether she had done it in her rush to search for Augusten, if Seth had come home and was waiting to do her bodily harm, or if Marnie had absent-mindedly forgotten to close the door. Either way, she knew to tread lightly as she entered the living room. With her hand poised on the mace resting at her hip, she tentatively opened the screen door and went inside. The lights in the kitchen and living room were on, but no one was in either room. Lenore knew better than to call out to her roommates, so she carefully sneaked toward her bedroom. Marnie's bedroom door was shut and the lights within were off, so Lenore knew that Seth's mother must have turned in for the evening. Lenore's bedroom door was slightly cracked and the light was off, so she reached into the open space with her free hand and groped around for the light switch. Once the light was on, she slowly opened the door and glanced around. Seth was nowhere to be found and there was no place he could hide in the cramped quarters. Content that she was safe, Lenore closed the bedroom door and pushed the bed up against it as a barricade.

*I won't let these people take me alive,* she vowed, grabbing a pillow and propping it up against the side of the bed to use as a sit-upon. She took the can of mace from its holster and shook it a few times before placing it back at her side. Taking her place on the pillow, she sat cross-legged and listened cautiously for the return of her deranged significant other, but ended up falling in and out of consciousness until she finally fell asleep, once again seeing Augusten in her dreams.

Lenore found herself at The Edge of Heaven once more, but the walls were made of glass that let the sickening pink and orange sunset leak into the nightclub. She saw Augusten in the crowd and they reached for each other again. His fingertips gently brushed the curve of her cheek, causing her to bashfully turn her head away, but he had turned into Seth when she looked at him again. The rest of her dream was disjointed—there were people from her church and people she had never seen before in her waking hours, and the setting continually changed venues until she woke up, disoriented and disappointed. *Damn it,* she thought, *I had hoped that the events from yesterday were all just one big nightmare.*

Lenore's head ached from the combination of stress and disordered sleeping. The knife wound on her side was not as painful as before; it only hurt when she applied direct pressure to the injury. Her throat was dry and scratchy, which meant that she must have fallen asleep with her mouth open at some point, and she felt dehydrated. Seth had left his water cup on the night stand, so Lenore picked it up and drank the remains of the ice cubes that had melted overnight. It was a scant refreshment, but she knew it would have to suffice until it was safe for her to leave the bedroom. She checked the window to see if anyone suspicious was roving around, but once again the streets were empty. She laid down on the bed, perpendicular to the mattress as not to dirty the sheets with her shoes, and hoped to regain some of her energy through a more comfortable rest, but she was too apprehensive to sleep. When her restlessness finally won out, she moved the bed back to its original position and slowly creaked the bedroom door open.

Marnie's bedroom door was still closed, which gave no indication as to whether she was out in the kitchen or still asleep. Lenore crept toward the living room and peeked through the entrance, finding Seth sitting on the couch with his head in his hands. He emitted a slow and quiet sob, and when he moved his hands away Lenore could see that his face was red from crying. She slowly entered the living room and approached him, but she stopped when he noticed her.

"My mom is in the hospital," he mourned.

Lenore stood at ease. "What happened?"

"I don't know." He wiped his eyes with his shirt. "I got a call from them while I was out last night, and by the time the paramedics got there, she had gone into a coma."

*The ambulance I saw last night...that must have come for Marnie.* Lenore wanted to ask Seth about Augusten, but did not want to further upset him. After all, if he was dangerous on a regular day, he would be even more so when emotionally compromised.

"I don't know what to do," Seth continued sobbing. "What if she dies? I can't pay for this place alone..."

Lenore rolled her eyes. *Of course that's the first thing you think of.* "Do you know what condition she's in right now?"

"I don't know." He sniffed and blew his nose into his hands, which he then looked at in disgust. He reached over to the comfortable chair and wiped his hands under the arm rest. "I don't want to be alone right now…"

Reluctantly, Lenore sat down near him on the opposite end of the couch. "Is there anything I can do?"

Seth shook his head. "Just…be with me right now."

Lenore looked down at her lap. *Augusten's still out there…I hope he's all right.* She thought of her prayer from the previous night. *No…I know he's all right. Wherever he is, he's in God's hands now.*

Seth glanced over at Lenore. "Will…will you come closer?" He held out his arms for a hug. Lenore just stared him down coldly, realizing that after everything that had transpired between the two of them, she legitimately did not care about his feelings. Ironically, it was likely the first time he had ever experienced something that was acceptable to be upset over. Nevertheless, she moved closer to Seth and allowed him to embrace her. He squeezed her tightly, causing her to cry out as he rubbed against the spot where the knife had grazed her.

"Are you all right?" He pulled away abruptly and lifted her sweatshirt. The bloodstain had long since dried, sticking to her wound at the point where the blade had sliced through the fabric.

Lenore narrowed her eyes at him. "I liked this shirt."

Somehow, the implied concern over her ruined T-shirt seemed to comfort Seth, perhaps reminding him of his mother. He put his arms around her shoulders. "I'll get you a new one."

Lenore tentatively placed her hands around Seth's back and rubbed it encouragingly. "Don't worry, bro—your mom will be okay." Secretly, she was glad the vindictive wretch of a woman was gone. If she managed to survive her predicament, then Lenore faced certain eviction from the apartment complex, and there was nowhere left for her to go. Besides, if Marnie's hospitalization was a direct result of Lenore's verbal attack, then it was only fair that Lenore took from Seth the person who mattered most to him when he had done the very same to her. In the end, though, none of that truly mattered to Lenore. All that she knew was that the one person who had given her hope throughout her time in that strange realm —her friend, her muse, her kindred spirit—was gone, and without him, there was nothing left to hold Lenore back from watching the world burn. She was no longer afraid of Marnie, which she had demonstrated the previous night. Without his mother around to protect him, Seth was far less threatening and had a clear vulnerability to exploit. The last obstacle for Lenore to face before she could finally cut out all of the toxicity in her life was the so-called "church" that had held such a foreboding presence in her life, and she silently pledged to take on that challenge as soon as the opportunity presented itself.

Just then, there was a knock at the door.

# CHAPTER TWELVE

The newest missionaries were a couple of young white men who could have been twins, save for one being slightly shorter than the other and covered with freckles. Lenore did not bother trying to read their name tags, or even check to see if the name tags were properly pinned to their dress shirts. They stared wide-eyed at Lenore, who looked absolutely frightening with her frazzled hair, smeared makeup, and visibly bloodstained T-shirt. Nevertheless, the freckled Elder stood by his conviction and prepared to deliver his sales pitch. "Good morning. Do you have a moment to share a message about Jesus Christ?"

"I know why you're really here." Lenore stood imposingly in the doorway, her hands resting on either side of the frame as though she could tear it in half on a whim. "You and the others are here to keep tabs on me—to make sure I'm living according to the law of the church. You think I'm slipping…you're here to screw with my sanity, make me feel guilty…"

The missionaries cringed slightly, but tried their best to stay collected. "We're just dropping by to see if there's anything you need," the taller Elder said evasively.

"I'll tell you what I need. I need *answers.*" Lenore stood up straight. "I want to know a few things, but I don't know if you're equipped to answer them."

"Well, if you have any questions," the freckled Elder piped up, "we'll be more than happy to try and answer them for you."

"And if we can't answer them now," the taller Elder added, "we'll pray about it and do our best to get back to you on it."

Lenore smiled. "Okay then…where to start?"

The missionaries noticed Seth sitting forlornly on the couch in the background. "Is that your husband?" the freckled Elder asked.

Lenore glanced behind her to see Seth curled up in the fetal position in his spot, clearly not in any mood to be hassled by religious solicitors. "Who, him? No." She screwed up her courage and looked the missionaries directly in the eye. "I'm not married, and I've no intention to be."

Both missionaries were dumbfounded by the revelation. "But… you've been living with this man?"

"He's not much of a man," Lenore corrected them, "but yes. For a time, we were in a relationship."

The freckled Elder fumbled about with a pen he had pulled out of his shirt pocket while the taller Elder glanced around awkwardly. "And you say you've been a member of the church for *how* long?" asked the latter.

"Gosh, I don't know…" Lenore moved her fingers as she counted silently in her head. "Two years, I think? I have no concept of time anymore."

The taller Elder scratched his head. "Well, this poses a problem with the Law of Chastity. Do you think we could have you schedule a time to come and confess this to the bishop?"

"Confess to the bishop?" Lenore repeated. "You mean, like a Catholic?"

The freckled Elder gave off a noticeable shudder at the mention of the alternative Christian denomination. "Well, not quite," he explained. "You see, from my understanding, when you talk to your leader in a different church, they give you a set of prayers to say, and supposedly, you are forgiven. But in the Lord's *true church*, there may be disciplinary measures taken. You may risk disfellowshipping, or even excommunication depending on the seriousness of the sin."

The taller Elder glared at his companion as though he had given Lenore too much information, but he remained tactful. "We'll set you up with an appointment to talk to the bishop. You can ask your questions then."

With that, they exchanged goodbyes as a mere formality, and then the missionaries went about their business. Lenore closed the door behind her and looked over at Seth, who had gone to sleep. She took off her sweatshirt and used it as a makeshift blanket to cover his torso, then went to the bathroom to clean herself up for the day.

Lenore took a long shower, carefully cleaning the knife injury and seeing that it was actually much smaller than she had anticipated. As the hot water washed away the dried blood and action grime from her olive skin, she began to wonder if she had done the right thing by telling the missionaries the truth about her relationship with Seth. *If I had just told them the truth from the beginning, I would not be in this mess. Augusten would still be here…and what's more, he might be with me at this very moment.* She hugged her naked body momentarily, trying to imagine what it might feel like to have him caress her subtle curves with his large hands, but the thought was too depressing to be arousing since she knew it was a shameful desire that would never come to pass. When she finished her shower, she used her index finger to longingly doodle a heart with her and Augusten's respective initials in the steam on the mirror. After admiring it for a moment while she toweled off, she committed it to memory and erased it.

While changing into fresh clothes in her bedroom, Lenore stashed the bloodstained T-shirt away in one of her drawers, as she was not ready to wash away the last remaining evidence of Augusten's existence. The bedroom door creaked open as she was pantless, prompting her to quickly dart for cover. "I'm indecent!" she shouted, which only provoked a lewd smile from Seth as he entered the room.

"Actually, I came in here for my water glass." He retrieved the glass from its place on the night stand, but lingered to watch Lenore finish dressing.

"Do you mind?" Lenore did not even look up at him as she slipped into a fresh pair of jeans.

"What's wrong? You used to let me watch you change, even with your whole celibacy thing."

"Letting you watch and being comfortable changing in front of someone are two different things." She zipped up her jeans. "How much did you hear when I was talking to the missionaries?"

Seth sat down on the bed. "Nothing, really…everything is just kind of passing me by right now. Why do you ask?"

"Well, they want me to go in and talk to the bishop about something."
"When?"

"Not sure. They said they'd contact me when they had more info."

"Well, they're certainly good at *that*." Seth rolled his eyes. "Shouldn't they make you sign some sort of waiver that they're going to give out your contact information to the whole damn congregation when you get baptized? I mean, I'm no Christian, but I don't remember the part of the Bible where Jesus said 'thou shalt have no privacy' or whatever."

Lenore forced a smile at Seth's attempted joke. "Well, I'm sure their hearts were in the right place. But yeah, I'm not too sure about all that." She decided not to tell Seth about the possibility of leaving the church, in order to avoid both the unwanted expectation of sexual favors and the chance of him becoming volatile once he knew that the wedding was off.

They continued to make casual conversation well into the afternoon for what felt like the first time in months. Lenore was sure that having Marnie out of the picture released a huge burden from Seth's back, as he seemed humbled by the experience of losing access to his mother, but she could not forgive him for what he had done to Augusten. She dared not bring up the man in question, lest she evoke Seth's violent rage once more, but she still had a faint glimmer of hope that Augusten had somehow survived the attack and received help. Either way, she had every intention of avenging her dear friend, no matter who barred the way.

Lenore spent the following week anticipating when the missionaries would come back with news from the bishop. *Perhaps it was an empty threat, or maybe they forgot...they probably have a lot of people to keep tabs on.* Deep down, she still wanted to believe that the church was true, that it could be her way out of purgatory, but something in her core told her that there was no logic in the lessons they preached. What was once her source of refuge had become a soul trap; the congregation she had once been willing to sacrifice her personal happiness for meant nothing after her happiness had been forcefully taken from her. *Come what may...I'm ready for my disciplinary counsel.*

Marnie was still in the hospital, and Seth went to see her after work when he could spare the opportunity, going less often as he found new ways to enjoy his freedom. He mostly left Lenore to her own devices, only expecting her to eat dinner and watch television with him. She would have been satisfied merely to eat and return to her responsibilities, but it was a small sacrifice to make for her temporary security. Without Marnie around to keep her on edge, Lenore had more free time to use at her leisure, mostly reading her scriptures and taking down notes for the questions she wanted to ask the bishop.

Another Sunday came and went. Lenore did not go to church, but her presence went strangely unnoticed by the congregation. It was not until the following Wednesday that Lenore finally heard back from the church, when a thin, balding man with round eyeglasses and a leather-bound ledger came to her door. "Hello," he greeted. "May I please speak with Lenore...*Kavaranian*?" He clearly had trouble pronouncing her surname, but he managed to say it correctly the first time.

"This is she," Lenore responded.

"I'm the stake president, Adam Christensen," he introduced himself. "I understand you have some issues with the church?"

"I have some questions to ask, yes."

"And have you spoken with your bishop yet?"

"Not yet. The missionaries said that they would arrange for me to speak with him, then get back to me. That was over a week ago."

President Christensen perused his ledger. "My understanding is that you were to speak with the bishop on Sunday, and he would talk to me about whether or not you would need further guidance..." He glanced back at Lenore. "So, I take it you haven't been given your court date?"

"Court date?" Lenore's eyes widened. *What the hell did I do this time?*

"A stake disciplinary council is sometimes referred to as a 'court of love,'" President Christensen explained, trying to sound as nonthreatening as possible. "That is to say, it's not a meeting where you are to be judged for your sins, but rather an...*intervention,* of sorts. We will discuss the nature of your sins, and then decide what the best course of action will be."

"I see," Lenore replied, although she really did not understand the vagueness of President Christensen's explanation. "And what should I do in order to prepare for this?"

"Well, when you go to church the next few Sundays, we ask that you not partake in the sacrament as part of your repentance process. In the meantime, just keep reading the scriptures and praying...and it would probably be best to stop doing the thing you're being called to the council for." He adjusted his glasses. "My calendar says that your appointment is set for the last Wednesday of the month, around seven in the evening at the stake center. You know where that is, right?"

"No, I've never been there."

President Christensen gave Lenore some brief directions to the church's official business building. "Be sure to wear church dress, you know, a conservative dress, shoes...that sort of thing."

"Okay, I can do that."

"All right, then. Nice meeting you, Sister Kavaranian. I'll see you then."

"You too. I'll see you later."

Once President Christensen had left the area, Lenore turned away with a devious smile. *Now, we play the waiting game.*

The weeks leading up to her council were uneventful. Marnie remained in the hospital with no word on how long she was expected to continue surviving, and there was still no sign of Augusten, leading Lenore to consider the idea that she might never see him again. She did not bother going to church during that time, as there was no point to showing up just to refuse the sacrament and gain the curiosity of the entire congregation, though members would periodically come to see her and check on her well-being. Naturally, she told them nothing about her situation; she dismissed them all with the same vague assurance that everything was fine. When Sundays came around, she disappeared into the open to find any semblance of God, anything that would renew her broken spirituality, but she no longer knew what to look for.

On the Sunday before her scheduled disciplinary council, she walked out to the park where she had encountered Augusten the last time she had seen him. She sat beneath the big tree that had become her favorite thinking totem and tried to pray, but the thoughts would not come together. The sky was a grungy shade of teal, almost a reflection of the tarnished perfection she had grown accustomed to. However, the world around her was rather serene for once, with a gentle ambiance of crows and the occasional car cruising by on the street. Lenore closed her eyes and let her body sink into the soft grass, wishing she could go back to being a child at her grandparents' house, safe from her father, safe from her past lovers, safe from the Horvitzes…safe from the judgment of purgatory that she was not likely to survive. *If I could go back to 2012, or even back to living with my mom and Armin…even that would be preferable to this. If I could just die right now, just melt into this scenery…I could accept that, and finally be at peace.*

Suddenly, Lenore sensed a shadow passing over her eyelids. She opened her eyes to find a large yellow butterfly with black stripes and a swallowtail hovering overhead. *That butterfly!* She abruptly sat up and followed its flight pattern with her eyes. *Every time I've seen that type of butterfly, it was when I was at my most distraught…and only since I've been in purgatory.* She watched the creature disappear into the tree above, then stood up. *And every time I've seen it, I've gotten this feeling that everything is going to work out.*

The fateful Wednesday finally came around. Lenore had suffered through a restless night, plagued by subconscious anticipation for the meeting to come, but by the afternoon she was high on adrenaline, waiting anxiously for her moment of truth. She took the bus to the stake center, following the directions as dictated by President Christensen, and arrived a half hour early. The sky began to fade into the nauseating pink and orange sunset that foreshadowed a potential tragedy, but Lenore was more confident than ever. Dressed in her demure Sunday attire, she passed through the double doors of the church building, notes carefully tucked away in a binder, ready for whatever consequences awaited her.

Lenore had not been given any further instructions as to what room to be in or whom to look for, so she wandered about aimlessly until she encountered an official-looking gentleman in the hall and decided to ask him for help. "Excuse me, can you tell me how to get to the disciplinary council room?"

The man looked uncomfortable at having been asked for such a favor, but he politely replied "Right this way" and showed her to a room with a closed door. He knocked twice and then opened the door, gesturing for her to go through. Lenore thanked the man and entered the room.

The room in question was empty save for a long collapsible table set with six folding chairs on either side, some spare folding chairs toward the back of the room, and a brown wooden podium at the far end of the table. Twelve unfamiliar men sat around the table, while the bishop sat toward the back wall. President Christensen and two other strange men stood at the podium, waiting patiently for the woman of the hour. The walls were bare and white, which was further reflected by the flood of fluorescent lighting that seemed apropos of the bureaucratic environment, and the carpet was a dull brown that could almost pass for mauve. President Christensen beckoned for Lenore to come to the table, and as she did, all the seated men in the room stood up. The bishop placed a folding chair at the empty end of the table and motioned for Lenore to sit down in it. She quietly thanked him and complied.

"Thank you for joining us, Sister Kavaranian," President Christensen greeted. The other men sat down. "We would like to begin this council with a prayer." He and the other men bowed their heads and folded their arms, and Lenore followed in their example. "Our kind and gracious Heavenly Father, we thank thee for this opportunity to meet today and participate in these proceedings. Please bless us that we may be guided to judge fairly, that we may feel thy spirit upon us as we come to a decision regarding the situation at hand. We ask these things in the name of thy son, Jesus Christ. Amen."

The other men each chimed in with their own "Amen" and Lenore mumbled a subtle "Amen" after them. President Christensen cleared his throat and shuffled the paperwork on his podium. "Sister Kavaranian, we are meeting here tonight on behalf of our Lord and Savior to hold this disciplinary council for you, on the accusation that you have willfully violated the Law of Chastity. The possible consequences of this violation may result in no action or formal probation, or if found to be more serious, disfellowshipping, or even excommunication. Do you admit or deny your participation in this misconduct?"

Lenore looked up at President Christensen, completely emotionless. "Will I have a chance to state my case regardless of my plea?"

"Sister Kavaranian, please answer the question."

"Admit." She gave no hint of either arrogance or remorse in her voice, leaving the brethren puzzled as to how to continue their proceedings.

"All right, then." President Christensen folded his hands over his paperwork. "Sister Kavaranian, will you please describe the nature of your transgression?"

Lenore swallowed dryly. "When I was baptized a member of the church, I mistakenly led the missionaries to believe that I was legally married to my then-boyfriend. I continued to sell that lie after I was baptized, with the intent of marrying him in private at a later date."

"And during this time, did you have sexual relations with your boyfriend?"

"No, I did not. I actually did follow the Law of Chastity in that regard, and he respected my request under the premise that we would elope within a matter of months."

President Christensen was taken aback. "So, you are saying that you did not act inappropriately with your boyfriend after becoming a member of the church. Are you taking into account any other acts of indecency, such as oral sex, autoerotic stimulation, heavy petting…anything of that nature?"

"I did not."

"Well, what about before you became a member?"

Lenore raised an eyebrow. *Not even my gynecologist would ask me this much about my sex life.* "My intimate involvement with my boyfriend prior to my membership with this church has already been accounted for during my baptism."

"Sister Kavaranian, please do not evade the question. We are here to offer you assistance in your repentance process."

"My repentance process should be between me and God, just as the scriptures say." Lenore narrowed her eyes, and her offense became audible. "In fact, this is part of those questions I had regarding church doctrine, the ones I was told *by you* that I would be given answers for in this meeting."

President Christensen was noticeably irritated, but he also seemed to be nervous about Lenore's unyielding resolve. "We have come here to discuss your transgressions—"

"And I'm *discussing* them," Lenore interrupted. "And rather than discussing the lurid details, I think it would be more logical to discuss my reasoning *why* I made these…transgressions, as it were."

President Christensen prepared to argue, but some unseen force held him back. "Very well."

Lenore opened her binder, using her notes as a guide. "It is my understanding, given the words of contemporary prophets both past and present, that marriage is a commandment of God—and yet his own son, Jesus, was never married in his lifetime. Given that he was still baptized in spite of his sinless nature, purely to set the example for mankind to follow, would it not make sense that he would follow this ancient commandment? Likewise, Paul the Apostle never married either, even spoke cynically on the subject, and he is credited as being the one to popularize Christianity as a whole. My first question is this: has marriage always been a commandment, and if not, why did God suddenly make it so?"

The men in the room looked confusedly at one another. One of the men whispered something to President Christensen, which he then repeated. "The commandment of marriage has always been part of our Heavenly Father's plan of happiness for us. Why would an obedient servant of the Lord choose not to follow one of his commandments?"

Lenore's eye twitched at the stupidity of the circular logic. "That doesn't answer my question at all."

"Well then, perhaps you should pray about it, and the answer will be revealed to you."

"Is this some kind of joke?"

"Sister Kavaranian, I assure you this is a grave matter."

"I understand that. And that's part of my next question: considering that the commandment of eternal marriage is necessary for salvation, and this worthiness is determined at the discretion of the church—as is the example here and now—who are we, as people on Earth, as mere mortals, to determine the fate of one's salvation? It's been my understanding thus far that God alone determines the fate of one's soul, but assuming this church is true, then how is it part of God's plan that the higher authorities of the church—with all do respect, brethren—have the power to block someone from said salvation?"

"I'm sorry, I don't understand your question."

"Okay, let me rephrase that." Lenore thought for a moment, then came up with a parable. "Say a law was passed that allowed two people of the same sex to legally marry. This would go against church doctrine, so say the church presidency passed a policy saying that any children that were legal wards of one of these couples could not participate in any saving ordinances, like baptisms, until they themselves became adults. If no one can get to the highest tier in heaven save for having these ordinances done, and these innocent children should die before reaching adulthood, then the church has effectively created a caste system of souls, which does not sound like something a forgiving God would do."

The brethren began murmuring among themselves, creating a dull buzz that blended hushed words into pure noise. The walls began to separate into squares, varying from their original bright white to a moderate shade of gray. One by one, each man in the room began to fade from view. The bishop was the first to disappear completely, gone before President Christensen could open his mouth to address Lenore.

"Sister Kavaranian," President Christensen began as the rest of the brethren gradually vanished, "I am afraid this is worse than I thought. You appear to be acting in apostasy..." He disappeared entirely, but his voice remained to continue, "...and you will await further judgment."

The room was empty, and Lenore was alone. The walls faded away to reveal the pink and orange sunset, and Lenore knew that she had overcome another major trial.

# CHAPTER THIRTEEN

The sunset continued well into what should have been night, leaving the sky aggressively pink even after Lenore finally made it home. Despite having walked back the entire way, she was filled with anxious energy. *It's time to strike while the iron is hot,* she said to herself determinedly. She had already defeated two impossible obstacles that she had long feared she would be subservient to forever, but still had some unfinished business to attend to. *Now...where is Seth?*

Lenore found him watching television in the living room once more. "I'm back," she announced, and he turned to greet her.

"How was it?" he asked.

"It was...liberating." Lenore smiled her first real smile since Augusten's tragic fate several weeks prior.

"Liberating? How so?"

"Well...let's just say I feel closer to God now more than ever before."

"Sounds good. Tell me more about it later."

"Okay." Lenore was relieved that she did not have to relay the events of the court of love to Seth right away, as she was not emotionally equipped to handle another argument with someone so woefully oblivious to the feelings and sufferings of others. She headed for the bedroom to change out of her church clothes once and for all.

Lenore opened her dresser drawer and retrieved the bloodstained T-shirt with the strawberry on the front. *We did it, Augusten,* she thought as she held the shirt open lovingly. *We're free.* She hugged the shirt tightly as she savored the memory of her lost companion one last time. *I'm sorry I couldn't save you...but now I'm going to find the way out of here myself.* She put on the dirty shirt, along with a fresh pair of jeans. Her black pageboy cap and the belt with the holster of mace completed her ensemble, and after slipping her shoes on she left the apartment without saying goodbye to Seth. He ignored her in favor of focusing on his television program, which segued into a sex scene by the time the screen door closed behind her.

The sky still held tight to its violent pink and orange hues, but had become peppered with yellow clouds tinged with gray at the bottoms.

Lenore thought that it looked like an artist's abstract rendition of abdominal viscera, which was fitting as she was, in her mind, centrally located in the bowels of purgatory. A quick glance out toward the back gate showed that there was nothing out there but open sky, and a brief walk to check outside of the front gate resulted in the same. Lenore looked up at the buildings, which seemed to be stretching increasingly higher, at least twice as many stories tall as they were originally. *There's no way out of here…this is it. This crapsack apartment complex is where my time in purgatory ends.*

A yellow butterfly with black stripes, which Lenore had become accustomed to seeing at crucial moments in the fight for her sanity, flew in front of her from an unknown entrance in the atmosphere. *I've seen this same type of butterfly several times now, each time being a point when I think I'm at my lowest, and this butterfly has always proven to be some sort of sign from God…* Suddenly, Lenore recalled some significant words Augusten had shared on the night of the dinner party, the night that she had started to fall in love with him: *"They say that God works in mysterious ways, but maybe it's more like subtle ways. Maybe we need to find our own way to God…or recognize the signs when he finds us."* At last, Lenore understood: *God is all around us. He never left us; we took his existence for granted. He will show us peace, but we have to be open to the signs around us. We can't let someone else tell us how to get to God…we have to find him in our own way.* She followed the butterfly as it danced in the sky, heading toward the back gate and the two mystical evergreen trees. *Or maybe we just have to be open-minded enough to see the signs when he comes for us.*

Lenore continued to track the butterfly's erratic flight pattern, trudging along the sidewalk slowly as though in a trance. She started up one of the impossibly long staircases, not noticing that they continued to expand after her ascent until the butterfly disappeared into the yellow clouds above. The clouds began to converge at the center point between the two tapered evergreens. As Lenore watched the clouds shift, she felt a burning in her bosom that granted her the premonition that anything yellow she could see was the presence of God. *Thank you for finding me,* she prayed as she climbed higher. *And now, it's my turn to find you.*

By the time Lenore made it to the first landing, she was certain that she was well above where the roof of the complex should be, even though there was still a long expanse of stairs above her leading to the second floor. The two evergreens continued to stretch high up into the universe, but most of the remaining trees had stopped short of where Lenore stood. She could see the tops of their branches through the gaps left by the clouds as they drifted away, leaving just enough visibility to display a green patch of grass on the ground below. She was no longer sure that she was still on Earth, and if she was not, then where she was going was also unclear. Nevertheless, she pushed forward, determined to reach the center of the yellow cloud entity.

It was only when a flock of crows floated by at her eye level that Lenore's uneasiness set in. She paused momentarily and the clouds dispersed, showing that she was high above the common trees. The metal rail felt flimsy in her hand, and she slowly sat down on one of the steps. Watching the crows to take her mind off of her sudden vertigo, she took slow, deep breaths and wondered how much further she had to go in order to reach her destination. *I can't stop now, though. I've come too far, and there's nothing to go back to. I just have to have faith that whatever I'm reaching for will bring me the peace and understanding that I seek.* She cautiously rose again, squeezing her torso for comfort and catching a glimpse of her bloodstained T-shirt. *Augusten. It was you who kick-started my paradigm shift, and for that, I'm a better person. I owe it to you to find happiness.* She gently caressed the tear in her top and collected her bearings, then continued her quest to reach the summit of the apartment complex.

Suddenly, Lenore heard the sound of footsteps behind her. She did not turn around, lest she find another distraction to prevent her from achieving her goal. She was close to the second floor, or rather, that which was up higher than the second story of the complex, breaking through the dense patches of yellow fog that coasted through the atmosphere. *This is it. This is where I'm supposed to go.* The second floor was one step away when she felt an unknown force grab her from behind and pull her backward. Lenore screamed and struggled to pull away, turning her head to find out who or what had taken her.

It was Seth, and Lenore discerned that he must have been responsible for the footsteps she had heard behind her. "What are you doing?" he cried. "Are you trying to jump?"

"My business here is complete." Lenore contorted and shifted away from Seth's reach. "Don't you see what's happening here? It's over. Everything is ending."

Seth looked around, dumbfounded. "Are you having another religious hallucination?"

*Perhaps he doesn't see the same optical illusions I do,* Lenore considered. "Doesn't anything look different to you?"

"The sky is weird," Seth admitted. "And everything seems...I don't know, *larger* somehow. Or something like that."

"We're among the last people here. Everyone else is gone."

Seth's facial expression sobered as he pondered Lenore's statement, but she could not tell if he was actually coming to terms with the end of their time in purgatory or if he was trying to figure out what was wrong with her. "If we're the only ones left, then you're all that I've got." He attempted to seize her once more, but she hopped away, landing one step higher than him.

"You've taken everything from me," she declared. "You brought me to this miserable hellhole for your own selfish reasons. You allowed your mother to mistreat me for the sake of continuing your free ride. You *murdered* the person I cared about most—in front of me, no less—out of a jealous suspicion."

"Never mind that I turned out to be right about it, you whore."

"Nothing happened between me and Augusten, and you made sure that nothing will. And yet, it doesn't make me love you. You wasted all this time on me, and you could have found someone else—"

"Why, so they could do the same?" He took a half-step toward her, and she poised her hand above the holstered mace.

"If you think that, then why bother with a relationship at all? And why *me*, of all people?"

"Because, I *wanted* a relationship. And I wanted it with *you*. You're supposed to be my wife, after all." He reached out to grab her again.

Lenore immediately tore the can of mace from its holster and sprayed him in the face, all in one clean motion. She quickly moved her head away from the chemical cloud, as not to accidentally breathe in her own self-defense mechanism, and ducked away. Seth stumbled backward, choking on the spray. While he was disoriented, Lenore push kicked him in the chest, causing him to tumble down the stairs.

"I'm not your wife," she called out as an afterthought, "and I refuse to enter eternity with you!"

Seth rolled down the stairs until he hit the landing, falling a great distance away from Lenore. When his momentum finally stopped, he let out a pained shriek, and Lenore could see that his right arm was mangled in an unnatural direction. He tried in vain to sit up, wriggling like a worm and succeeding only in raising the right half of his upper body, resting his weight on his undamaged left arm.

"You fucking *bitch!*" he screamed to the best of his ability, his voice unnaturally high and scratchy from the results of the defensive attacks. He repeated those and other vile epithets over and over, but eventually the screeching of his mantra became a single high-pitched note that Lenore was able to tune out. She looked down at him and he gradually became smaller as the second landing began to rise, allowing her to clearly see the cloud congregation between the two tapered trees. Suddenly, Lenore saw the butterfly again, appearing out of a nearby cloud and fluttering around her head for a moment before flying toward the two trees, subconsciously prompting her to follow it.

*I know what I have to do.* Lenore carefully climbed up on the narrow rail, somehow maintaining a balance on the thin metal strip. When the butterfly vanished into the cloud cluster, Lenore jumped forward, reaching for the wispy yellow formations, and gently fell like a leaf dropping from a tree. As she coasted downward, she felt several warm gusts of wind pushing her upward, keeping her in suspended animation as the yellow clouds swirled about her entire body. She looked upward, seeing the two evergreens on either side of her, and watched as a myriad of small white stars appeared at random in the hot pink sky. The gentle motion of the wind and the soothing presence of the clouds relaxed Lenore, and she closed her eyes, finally feeling at peace. The yellow clouds surrounding Lenore's body drifted outward as she lay haphazardly on the concrete below, leaving dark red streaks behind to stain the sidewalk beneath her. The apartment complex faded back to its regular proportions, and the sun faded below the horizon.

After what seemed like hours, Lenore felt her body rise upward once more, prompting her to open her eyes. She turned over weightlessly to see the ground below her and watched the apartment complex shrink from view, but the two trees continued to stretch into space. By the time Lenore was able to see the tops of the roofs, she realized that it truly was just a single open box in a vast universe. She continued to rise above the apartment complex until it began to morph from a square to an oblong shape, and the two tapered evergreen trees shrank down into the oblong until they completely disappeared.

The salmon pink of the buildings and green of the foliage blended together as a wave of red seeped in, boiling like a giant cauldron. Suddenly, various figures from Lenore's pre-purgatory life emerged from the cauldron: John, Alicia, Piper, James, and Matt, all naked and intertwined with one another. Matt was sodomizing John, who was penetrating Alicia from behind, who was groping Piper, who was fellating James, who in turn began to fondle Matt—all of whom were unwilling participants with one another, but unable to escape the debauchery. Lenore observed the scene in horror. *This is the path they chose, and this is their hell to live out. They weren't great people...but it pains me to see them suffering like this.* Demonic-looking beings bubbled out from the cauldron to overtake the damned souls and join in the orgy of suffering, then all of them merged within each other, and Lenore floated away before she could see what was to become of them.

Lenore knew that there were separate hells that awaited the other people in her life, and one by one, these places were revealed to her. She saw Seth and Marnie continuing their parasitic relationship in a lower middle-class hellhole. Marnie could not control her compulsive spending and Seth was unwilling to stop her, even though every single expense of his that was met by his mother filled him with guilt. She saw her own mother and Armin in a similar situation, with her mother too mentally weak to overcome her crippling expenses and angry about the burden of such placed upon her. Lenore watched the two parent-and-child duos succumb to the misery of not having enough due to the unwillingness to sacrifice or lack of motivation, respectively. Again, she felt pity for them, even desired to help them, but she had already learned from her experience in life that she could not simultaneously give to them and save herself. All she could do was continue to have faith that they and her other adversaries could find a catalyst to overcome their tribulations. Lenore drifted away once more.

Lenore watched the universe expand before her in a multitude of stars and planets. She tried to look at her hands, but she could no longer see her own body. As she drifted off into space, she felt at ease, and an old mantra came to mind: *I am the universe, and the universe is me.* She realized that she had played her part in the great game of life; she had been significant in God's plan without ever having to complete all the rites or rituals that the heads of various churches deemed necessary for salvation. Lenore had become one with the universe, and she thought, *This must be what it feels like to become one with God.* She felt her spirit spread out far into the cosmos, no longer able to feel the weight of her own breath or the beating of her heart, or the movement of her fingers and toes brushing against each other. The universe continued to expand, and her with it, until it reached a point where her spirit stopped in stasis and everything else stretched out until even the twinkling lights of the stars disappeared, leaving her floating in an empty black void. Suddenly, Lenore was filled with an overwhelming sense of fear.

*No,* she thought despondently, *this can't be! Is this…outer darkness? Am I here because I rejected the true church? Or am I here because I sold my soul to that church and took on their punishment and reward system to be my own personal hell?* Alone in the silent darkness, she could feel nothing but her own panicked emotions. She could no longer sense the presence of God, and wondered whether she would eventually fade from the plane of consciousness or merely drift forever in the lonely void. *If this is my fate…then I suppose I will finally have to accept it.*

Suddenly, Lenore saw a brilliant light radiating next to her. She moved toward it, and saw a bulky anthropomorphic form glowing neon white. In spite of the indistinct features, she recognized the figure as Augusten. Although he was devoid of all clothing, his skin was so bright that any defining sexual characteristics were impossible to make out. He was positioned as if he was sitting on an invisible bench, unmoving and concentrating on the void in front of him. Her spirit was instantly filled with love and ecstasy, having at last been reunited with her kindred spirit.

"Augusten!" Lenore attempted to call out, but she had no voice, or else her words were lost in the void of space. She looked at her hands and noticed that she could see her own body once again, and that her olive tan was glowing bright white as well. Like Augusten, the fluorescence had rendered her anatomically incorrect; her nipples and genitalia were obscured by the light emanating from her new form. She could not reach Augusten or contact him, and she had no way of knowing if he was aware of her presence. The two of them sat on nothing, as if stuck on the edge of the universe, outside of everything superficial, not subjected to any major catastrophes or crises—just two souls giving off intimate energy, neither one knowing how or when to proceed to something greater.

The stars slowly began to reappear in the void. They gradually expanded into a circular pattern, becoming brighter and more prominent as they radiated outward. Lenore and Augusten sat motionless as the mandala formed, watching the stars dance until their radial alignment was complete. The central stars began to fade as a humanoid apparition materialized from the center of the mandala. Lenore immediately recognized it as the common depiction of Jesus Christ, whom she had always been taught was her Lord and Savior. He, too, glowed white, but his radiance was more subtle and soft, and he wore a white robe that stopped just short of his sandal-clad feet. She knew that the Savior had finally come for her, and that all of her suffering was about to end.

The Savior reached out for Lenore, who sat mesmerized by his presence. She turned to Augusten, who continued to sit catatonically in space, and tried to gain his attention. She called out to him, once again unable to hear her own voice, and turned to reach for him. As close as he was to her, he was still just out of her reach, and thus all of her efforts to save him were in vain. Nevertheless, the Savior waited patiently with his hand outstretched, waiting for Lenore to take it.

At that moment, Lenore realized that it was not her place to try saving Augusten, and that it was out of her power to do so anyway. The Savior would come for him personally, if and when Augusten was ready to receive him. She took one final look at Augusten, then turned her attention toward the Savior. She took his hand and he pulled her to a standing position. Their eyes met, and the Savior looked upon Lenore with compassion and understanding as he pulled her forward, stepping backward into the mandala as the stars swirled into a vortex. He vanished into the vortex, still pulling her forward, and she followed willingly until she, too, disappeared. As she emerged on the other side, everything became white, and she finally lost consciousness.

# CHAPTER FOURTEEN

The morning sun glowed bright and warm, emitting a welcoming yellow light over the sacred beauty of a brand new day. The chatter of common brown birds and the gentle swishing of thick tree branches in the breeze filled the air with aural aesthetic. Heaven and Earth were new once more, though whether it was by the grace of God, the natural order of things, or yet another challenge in the purgatorial process was up for speculation. In any case, the new day brought forth the promise of happiness for all who might seek to claim it as their own. A nearby park filled with various trees made the perfect venue for anyone looking specifically to fulfill that goal. On that particular day, one such group of adults had come to that corner of nature to find solace from the rat race, led by none other than Lenore Kavaranian herself.

Lenore walked slowly through the public park, dressed modestly in a long black cassock with matching black canvas shoes, enjoying the presence of God through the glory of nature. She wore a large black backpack filled with scriptures from various world religions and enough sandwiches and bottles of purified spring water to feed her entire congregation of spiritual knowledge-seekers, who followed her diligently through the trees in search of a particular place to sit and worship. Among her followers were her high school colleague John DeLuna and his friends Piper, James, Alicia, and Matt; her mother and her brother, Armin; her college acquaintance Seth and his mother, Marnie; and various others who had heard of her notoriety as a wandering Universalist minister and come to gain and share knowledge with her little group. She came across a patch of wild violets, which she stooped down to admire briefly as the other group members followed her example. She found a purple flower on the ground that had come loose from its host, but was otherwise still fresh, and picked it up. Dusting it off carefully, she admired it in the glistening sunlight before fixing it into her shoulder-length black hair with a Bobby pin.

"Reverend Kavaranian?" Seth spoke up.

Lenore smiled. "You can call me Lenore. We're all equal in the eyes of our Creator."

"I'm sorry…*Lenore*?" He corrected himself.

"Go on. What is it?" She reverently folded her hands together in front of her body, poised to listen intently to what he had to say.

"I do enjoy being one with nature, but I was wondering…do you think that you will ever set up an actual meetinghouse for us to pray in? Like, in the event of a storm or something?"

"I prefer to experience the world as God intended," Lenore replied calmly. "I'm afraid that if we start meeting in a building, we'll become a proper church, and if we get too big, we'll lose sight of what we originally sought to gain." She turned to face the rest of the group. "When I die, I expect this congregation to disband, and if destiny beckons any of you, you might start a group of your own. Maybe you will even branch off on your own before my time is over, and I will move on to another town to spread what I know."

"I see." Seth smiled. "That's a pretty good idea."

"I rather like the idea of an ephemeral church," Armin added. "It kind of makes you think back to the times of the New Testament and stuff, you know? Like, when Jesus would walk around, preaching his gospel to all that were willing to listen."

"Speaking of which," James chimed in, "do you think we'll find anyone new to invite to our group today? The park is pretty empty."

"Hmm." Lenore pondered for a moment. "Well, it is a Sunday morning, and a lot of people are probably in traditional churches right now. But you never know. It's a rather auspicious day, don't you think?"

The group continued through the vast park, trekking across fields of soft green grass and tiny yellow flowers. Lenore spotted a butterfly—a large yellow insect with black tiger stripes and a swallowtail—and stopped to examine it. "Look at that, you guys."

"Whoa!" John narrowly dodged its attempted divebomb. "That thing's the size of a bird!"

"I remember back when I lived in New Mexico, there were huge flocks of monarch butterflies in my backyard during their migration season," Marnie mused. "It was one of my favorite times of year."

Lenore smiled at Marnie. "I've come to enjoy butterfly watching myself."

They all watched the butterfly dance in the air for a few minutes before it flew out of sight. Lenore felt a strange sensation after seeing the magnificent insect, like a premonition that she should follow it, or at the very least, travel in the same general direction. Without a word, Lenore started heading after the butterfly, and her congregation joined her pursuit.

Lenore had no memory of the person she had been in her previous life, at least, no more than any of her friends or family did. Nevertheless, she had retained a sense of awareness toward spiritual matters, and thus been called to share her gift with others while simultaneously receiving their insights. She had decided early on in her young life that she was destined to become a woman of God, and after studying the doctrine and covenants of various world religions, she found that the most logical course of action was to first take the common elements of all the belief systems, then take the unique ideas that promoted happiness and well-being while leaving the violent and exclusionary concepts behind. Although largely inspired by Christianity, which was the spiritual method she was most familiar with given her upbringing and location in the world, she created her own religion, in a sense—but she did not force her creed upon anyone who came to speak with her about spirituality. Instead, she maintained a dialogue with all interested parties, and every session concluded with at least one person discovering something new. Her little group had started with her mother and Armin, then expanded to other social circles and continued to grow exponentially.

The members of the congregation took their time walking toward their unknown destination, making careful observations about their surroundings. They happened upon an unusual tree with a green, spiny trunk and tiger-striped white flowers tipped with hot pink. Noticing that it was the only tree of its kind anywhere in the park, Lenore determined that it must be significant. "Let's eat lunch here," she suggested, letting her backpack slide off her shoulders before sitting down about six inches away from the base of the tree. As the others followed her example, she opened her backpack and began passing out submarine sandwiches and bottles of water to all who were willing to receive them.

"Should we have a prayer?" John asked.

"Yeah," Lenore agreed. "Let's all take a moment of silence to give thanks in our own way." They bowed their heads and closed their eyes for a minute or two, with some of the members opting to fold their arms or clasp their hands in reverence. Once everyone had finished saying their individual grace, they tore into their sandwiches hungrily.

Lenore swallowed her first mouthful and addressed the group confidently. "Now then, does anyone have an inspirational message to share?"

"Well," Piper began, "as you all know, I've been having some problems in my love life. My boyfriend didn't seem like he was all that interested in having a serious relationship, and I was just constantly eating my heart out over it, drinking to cope with the insecurity..." She gesticulated to accentuate her anecdote. "Then one day I thought to myself, 'What is it that I really want out of this relationship?' So I decided to distance myself from him for a while, maybe see if he noticed…I quit drinking and started doing yoga, and from there, I started getting back in touch with myself." She took a quick sip from her water bottle. "The journey isn't complete, but I've come a long way."

"I've been having a different experience with alcohol," John stated. "You see, one Friday night, after I got into another argument with my gramps, I decided to sit out on the patio with a cold one. So I've got this slight buzz, you know, and I'm feeling kinda mellow…and there's this, like, *chill* in the air, and I can see every star in the sky. And suddenly…I feel like I'm not alone anymore." He closed his eyes and tranquilly reminisced about his fond memory.

Lenore smiled and nodded. "It's pretty amazing how something can be beneficial to one person and harmful to another. I guess that goes to show that we weren't all meant to fit in one box, philosophically speaking."

"That's why I never really subscribed to any one religion before," Marnie quipped. "There are so many paths to enlightenment, and it's selfish to think that any one person has all the answers."

"I find it's best just to respect everyone's beliefs," Lenore's mother spoke up. "We may not agree with everything the other person says, but as long as that person isn't doing any harm to themselves or other people, then it's best to just let them be happy."

"Yes…I agree with all those things!" Lenore was ecstatic to be making such a positive impact on people, especially those she found to be kindred spirits. "And Piper, maybe you can show us some of that yoga you've been practicing after we've finished our lunch."

"Sure, I can do that," Piper agreed. "I'm not, like, a master yogi yet or anything, but I'll show you all what I've learned so far."

"Okay then. Sounds good to me." Lenore reached for her backpack and opened it up again, pulling out a large book of Christian scriptures. "Last week, I shared a few verses from the Dhammapada regarding the mind. Now, I'd like to share some quotes from the New Testament…" Clearing her throat, she began to read aloud from a bookmarked page. "This is from the Gospel of John: 'This is my commandment, that ye love one another, as I have loved you. Greater love hath no man than this, that a man lay down his life for his friends. Ye are my friends, if ye do whatsoever I command you. Henceforth I call you not servants; for the servant knoweth not what his lord doeth: but I have called you friends; for all things that I have heard of my Father I have made known unto you.'" Lenore closed the book of scriptures and looked out at her congregation once more. "This is one of my favorite passages out of any religious text I've read so far."

"That's beautiful," Piper cooed. "What exactly does that last part mean, though?"

"Well, the way I see it, it means that we are all equals in this group that we've formed," Lenore replied confidently. "And going even deeper, I'd say that we all reflect in each other what we see in ourselves."

"I like that," John said.

"Me too," Seth agreed. "I'm not entirely sure that I would have the courage to die for a friend, though."

"Perhaps you just need the right friends," John suggested. "I've known most of you guys for years, and after all we've been through, I think I'd have no trouble taking a bullet for any of you."

"But what if my friends do something wrong, or betray me?" Seth wondered. "How am I supposed to love them after that?"

Lenore spoke up softly. "We can't control the actions or feelings of others, and at times it may actually be necessary to distance ourselves from others in order to preserve our own well-being."

"That's what I had to do with Archer," Piper explained. "I still love him, but now it's more like I love him as a child of God than as a relationship partner. I wish him well in whatever he decides to do, and from here on out, I'm just gonna focus on bettering myself."

"Yeah," Lenore agreed, "I like the way Piper said it." Piper smiled graciously at the acknowledgment.

The congregation continued to feast on their sandwiches and bottled water, and Lenore once again took notice of the world around her. She spotted a large tree standing a short distance away, and sitting beneath the tree was a heavyset young man wearing a purple sweatshirt and baggy black jeans with the cuffs rolled up. He rested one arm on top of a large gray backpack, and it was difficult to tell if he was homeless or merely a student from the local community college, though given the day of the week he was more likely to be the former. Either way, Lenore was compelled to walk over to the man and invite him into her group. She set aside the remainder of her lunch and rose from her seat.

"Where are you going?" Seth inquired as Lenore set off to talk to the stranger.

"There's a man over there," she explained, "and I'm going to see if he wants to join us."

"Ah, okay." Seth beamed and took another bite of his sandwich. "Good idea."

"The more, the merrier!" Alicia agreed.

The congregation continued to chatter among themselves and enjoy their meal as Lenore gracefully approached the purple sweatshirt man. He sat solemnly beneath the tree, staring off into space as though consumed with a troubling thought, tapping his fingers rhythmically against his backpack. Upon closer inspection, she could see that he was listening to music through a pair of tiny ear buds connected to a small MP3 player.

"Excuse me." Lenore tried to gain his attention by waving her arm in his peripheral vision, and succeeded. "Is everything okay?"

"Yeah, I'm all right," he assured her, pausing his MP3 player and pulling out one ear bud. "Just enjoying nature."

Lenore smiled. "I came out to do the same thing, in a matter of speaking. It's part of how I connect with God."

The purple sweatshirt man removed his second ear bud and eyed her clerical garments. "So, you're a minister?"

"Technically, yes," she replied, smoothing out her cassock. "I'm ordained and all, but I feel that spreading the gift of God is something that anyone and everyone can aspire to do. I wear this garment as a means of letting people know that I'm available as someone who can offer guidance."

He cocked his head to one side in a display of curiosity. "You seem kind of young to be a preacher, though. How old are you?"

"Me? I'm not that young. I'm already twenty-five."

"That's my age as well. I'd say you're still young."

Lenore felt her face heat up from the compliment. "Well, I've known from an early age that I wanted to preach the good news."

"That's pretty neat. What church do you belong to?"

"Oh, I don't have a church, per se." Lenore shrugged to illustrate her point. "I just invite people to come join me in my spiritual quest, and we provide each other with insight on how we connect with God."

"I see." The purple sweatshirt man smiled. "I like that idea."

"Yeah. I believe that everyone has to find God in his or her own way."

"I agree. Or maybe, it's that God finds us..."

"...and we have to know the signs." They finished the thought simultaneously, then grinned shyly at one another. Lenore looked away bashfully for a second, then turned back to the man with a new light in her eyes.

"I'm Lenore, by the way. Lenore Kavaranian."

"Augusten Keys." He offered his hand for her to shake, and she accepted.

"Augusten." The purple sweatshirt man's name seemed to roll off of Lenore's tongue with the greatest of ease, as though it was a name she was meant to speak often. "I'll remember that name."

"Likewise. Good to meet you, Lenore."

"It's good to meet you, too." Lenore gently pulled her hand away, then pointed to her congregation, who were still eating and conversing joyfully. "I'm actually having a group meeting at this very moment. In fact, I came over to you in hopes that you would join us."

Augusten glanced briefly over toward the group of knowledge-seekers, then returned his attention to Lenore. "Well, I'm good over here for now. But I do appreciate the offer."

Lenore's heart fell slightly. "Are you sure? We have sandwiches, if you're hungry. And there's plenty to go around."

"It's okay, I've already had something to eat. Thanks anyway, though."

"Okay." Lenore turned to walk back to her group. "If you change your mind, you know where to find me. I'm in this park every Sunday morning, just so you know." She waved gently. "See you around, Augusten."

Augusten offered a vague wave in return. "Laters."

Lenore went back to her group, somewhat saddened, but also certain that her work was not yet finished. "He wasn't interested," she told the others.

"Aww, that's too bad," Alicia lamented.

"Not even for the sandwiches?" Matt exclaimed in disbelief.

"It's okay," Lenore assured the others. "Something in my core tells me that I haven't seen the last of Augusten." She sat down and resumed her place with the others as their spiritual guide.

Augusten listened to the low murmur of Lenore's ministry while lost in his own mind, most likely musing silently about his life. He picked up his ear buds again and started to place one in each ear, but decided against listening to music at the last minute and stared blankly down at the cords in his large hands. He glanced back toward the group with curiosity, then stood up, hoisting his backpack over one shoulder and pocketing the MP3 player and ear buds. After dusting off his legs and backside, he tentatively headed over to Lenore's group to take part in the shared celebration of newly discovered spirituality.

# ABOUT THE AUTHOR

S.E. Ramirez is an indie comic artist and writer. She graduated from Mt. San Jacinto College in San Jacinto, CA, with her Associates Degree in Art. She lives in Anaheim, CA.

www.ingramcontent.com/pod-product-compliance
Lightning Source LLC
Chambersburg PA
CBHW020253150626
46552CB00020B/795